MW01134670

To Maribeth

Brenda Spalding

Honey Tree Farm

By

Brenda M. Spalding

Heritage Publishing. US

ISBN-13: 978-1532897603

ISBN-10: 153289760x

This book is dedicated to all the hard working farmers, ranchers, and of course, the beekeepers, who settled rural Florida. I hope this book will help to tell their story.

The book is also dedicated my grandson, who loves the great outdoors and all its creatures.

Honey Tree Farm

*For the Love of a
Beekeeper's Daughter*

Honey Tree Farm

Chapter 1

Oh, Josh, can we really do this? I would love a break," called Maggie. She took the coffee carafe and poured two cups of coffee, adding sugar and a healthy portion of International Delight-Caramel Macchiato coffee creamer to hers.

"Coffee's ready," she said, as she carried them into the bedroom. She put his on the counter and took a sip of her own.

She finished getting ready for work, making the bed and picking up the few things scattered about the bedroom of the small condo she shared with her boyfriend, Josh Beaumont.

"It would be great to go to Florida. Just think; warm weather, sunshine, beaches and mojitos every evening."

"Sure we can," replied Josh, checking his reflection in the mirror and straightening his collar. "My parents would love to have us."

Josh had delighted Maggie - or Mary Margaret McDonald is what the plaque on her desk at work read - by suggesting the trip down to his parents' place in Sarasota for a week. The couple had not had have a vacation while Josh was in college and money was still tight. The student loans would take years to repay, but with his new job and her salary they would be relatively comfortable.

They turned out the light, took their coffee and moved into the small kitchen.

"I am looking forward to seeing you in that little bikini," Josh said.

"That sounds risqué," she replied, and cocked one eyebrow.

"I only meant you have an amazing figure, but now that you mentioned it, it is a *little* bikini.

"Oh, stop." She smiled and turned away.

Maggie was attractive, and at five foot seven, with dark auburn hair and blue eyes she turned the heads of men wherever she went. Josh counted himself lucky and it helped that he didn't have a jealous bone in his body.

"What are you thinking, Josh? You're positively leering at me."

"I was just thinking we might reenact the beach scene in the movie 'From Here to Eternity," he said, waggling his eyebrows Groucho Marx-style.

"You get me to Florida, and we just might do that," she exclaimed, throwing the dishtowel at him.

Josh had recently passed his bar exam, and there would be a few weeks before he started his new job. This trip would be a celebration and a little break before he started as an associate with the firm of Bates & Dunlop in Atlanta. Her job was Sales Analyst with First Federal Savings and Loan.

They had met when he went into her bank to open a checking account. It was an instant attraction. That was three years ago and they were very happy sharing the small - economical - condo on Peach Tree Street. It would not have been so comfortable if not for the fine restaurants and lounges nearby. Even the historic Fox Theater was within walking distance.

With some wheedling Maggie was able to rearrange her work schedule. Mr. Ambrose, her boss, had finally granted her the time off.

"You know, Maggie, you'd better come back. You've been with us quite a few years now and you've worked your way up the ladder." He used both hands to remove his glasses and held them to the light. He pulled a handkerchief from his pocket and polished the lenses. "Why, I remember when you started here. It was after high school and before you took those night classes at the college. Mr. Higgins, from the home office, was very impressed with you when he made his quarterly visit." Ambrose inspected the lenses again. Satisfied, he put them back on adjusting each arm of the thin wire frames.

"We think that with a few more courses you would be eligible for another promotion."

"I appreciate the compliment, and I will be back... don't you worry," she replied, with an easy smile.

When Maggie got home she and Josh began packing.

"I can't believe we got such a reasonable flight on such short notice," he said as he tossed his leather ditty bag onto the baggage.

"We can chalk that up to your detail-oriented, matter of fact, no nonsense, type-A personality, my dear Rhett" she said in a soft Southern drawl as she added their bathing suits to the pile in the suitcase.

"Why, Miss Scarlett, what about my manly charm and the charismatic influence that I have on women?" he asked with a mock drawl sounding more like Kentucky than the Old South.

She burst into laughter, and kissed him on the cheek. "If you ever thought of taking up acting... Don't!"

It was a mad dash to ATL through Friday evening traffic. When they finally made it to the airport Josh handed the cab driver an extra fiver since he'd made *almost* every light in route. Maggie hurried off to get in line at the baggage counter while Josh hurried to keep up. It was a case of 'hurry up - wait' avoiding collisions and dodging other travelers all rushing in different directions.

12

They made it to the gate just as the overhead voice announced their departing flight.

"I'm exhausted," Maggie said with a sigh. She took the center seat as Josh stashed their carry-on into the upper storage compartment before sliding into the aisle seat. "Airports exhaust me." She fumbled with the seatbelt and it finally clicked in place.

"Why don't you close your eyes and get a nap. We've got a short two hours before we land."

"Baby, you're the greatest..."

When Josh would later relate this experience to friends he would swear that she was asleep before she even finished the sentence.

Chapter 2

Josh picked up the rental car while Maggie freshened up. Although she'd met them a few times, it wouldn't do for Josh's parents to see her uncombed and unkempt.

"What did we get?" she asked, as they met at the exit. "I hope it's the blue Jaguar XE." She flashed a quizzical smile.

"Close. It's a red Ford Mustang V6."

"Perfect." She took his arm and they strolled through the line of cars with numbered sections, until they found the car that matched their ticket. They loaded up and put the top down before heading out the exit.

Tampa airport is well marked and they quickly found their way to the George J Bean Parkway and I-275 and over the Skyway Bridge.

"My parents came to Florida a lot when they were young. They drove, or flew sometimes. In the 80s there were twin bridges here," Josh began. "One day a barge missed the opening and hit the base somewhere in the middle. The twins were so steep that drivers couldn't see that the road had dropped away. Several went over and into the water below. They have a picture taken on their way back. All the traffic had been rerouted onto the surviving twin and the shot is of the broken bridge. It looked like a giant had taken a bite out of it. Mother was so frightened by the sight that she refused to take the Skyway Bridge again, until after they replaced them."

"When did they move here?"

"They sold the house in Atlanta and moved to Sarasota," he said, "sometime in the 90s. It was well after this bridge was built. They bought a great place behind the Ringling Museum that overlooks the bay."

Maggie laid her head back. The evening air was warm, unlike Atlanta in March. "I can't wait to see it." Suddenly, she seemed to remember something, took off her watch and reached for her purse.

"What are you doing?"

"Our vacation started when we landed..." She dropped it inside and put the purse on the floor again. "...and from this point on there will be no appointments or schedules; therefore, no clocks or watches."

"What if we make reservations at a restaurant?" he asked, aware that he was thwarting her plan.

"I hate it when you do that *devil's advocate* thing. However, in that case - we will make an exception." She laid her head back drawing in a long refreshing breath of the warm atmosphere.

Gary and Jean Beaumont had been able to retire early, thanks in part to very successful real estate businesses; first in Atlanta and then for several years in Florida. It was easy for them to sell sunshine to Floridians and northerners alike. They joined the local country club early on in order to meet, make friends and build an acquaintance base; potential clients. Now they were officially retired and spent their free time playing golf, boating, fishing and traveling.

Josh merged onto I-75 south. The sky was clear and once away from city lights Maggie could see the stars.

"You'll like staying with my parents. We can spend as much time on the beach as we like. My parents are always in and out. They keep a very active schedule."

"I look forward to relaxing, too. We can lie around the pool or take a dip in the ocean in the evening. There are a lot of choices. The sun will feel wonderful after Atlanta's cold winter.

"I called Mom and Dad and told them we had a late flight and not to wait up for us. But they will be there with the house lights on.

"Good. Maybe they'll some white wine chilled, too."

"No doubt."

It was almost 1:30am when they spotted the house.

"Let me guess," Maggie said. "It's the house with all the lights on; inside and out."

"You're good. I don't know how you do it." They both laughed.

The front door opened before they could get the key out of the ignition. By the time they opened the doors they could hear the happy chatter of the two senior citizens rushing toward them.

"Oh, good, you made it. How was the trip?" cooed Jean, who was still dressed in spite of the hour.

"Here, Son. Let me help you put the top up. You can never be sure if it'll rain this time of year."

The next half hour or so was filled with friendly conversations over white wine. Josh grinned, smiled at Maggie and cocked a perceptive eyebrow as if to say 'Told ya'.'

"I'm sure the kids are tired. Why don't we show them to their room and call it a night?" Gary suggested. "Tomorrow is almost here and we've got Pickle ball scheduled with the Bakers at 10am."

"That's a good idea," Jean agreed before bounding into her characteristic soft spoken, but rapid-fired way of speaking. "I left some brochures on the bureau for you to look through. Maybe you'll see something you like. Soap and towels are on the vanity in your bathroom. We won't wake you, in case you want to sleep in. Help yourself to anything you find in the fridge. Coffee will be ready for you on the counter."

"If you need anything, you can call us on our cells," Gary added, as he gently guided Jean out the door.

Chapter 3

Josh browsed through the brochures as Maggie poured them a second cup of coffee - hers with a hefty portion of International Delight, Hersey's Chocolate Carmel flavor coffee creamer - and his black.

"See anything interesting?" she asked, as she ran her fingers through her auburn hair. "It looks like it might rain."

"I noticed. Why don't we take a drive to Arcadia? It's very historical and old Florida. They have some great antique shops. Maybe we can find up something for the condo, you know, as a souvenir."

"You do realize that I must have been an interior designer in a previous life. I love nothing better than hunting for great objects."

"Then it's a plan," he replied. "There's a winery out that way, too. It's in one of these brochures. We can surprise Mom and Dad with a bottle for dinner tonight. Dad said they'd bring home some stone crabs, if the price is right."

"Mmm..., stone crabs and wine. That sounds so *Florida*. We can pick up some salad

19

makings on the way back too. If you'll Google
the winery, I'll clean up these dishes. It'll only
take a minute. We don't want to leave a mess
for your mom."

"Good idea, then we can take off." he
walked away.

"Oh, don't forget your cell phone. Mine is
still charging," she called after him.

I-75 was congested as usual this time of
year. They turned onto SR 70 and took the
exit east toward Arcadia before catching
Country Road 675.

"You were right suggesting we stop at the
winery first since it is closer." Maggie said, as
she watched for the road sign that would take
them to the Rosa Fiorelli Winery. "There it is.
Turn left there."

They pulled into the parking lot, tires
crunching on the crushed shell driveway.

"Oh, Josh, doesn't this look interesting? I
had pictured a replicated stone villa. This is a
more modern building, very industrial."

The parking lot was almost full with
license plates were from all over the US.
Many from Ohio, Illinois and Michigan.

"Look! There's one from California and
there's one from Texas," Maggie pointed at
the gold Cadillac with spoke wheel covers.

"Looks like the snowbirds have already
found this place."

"Uh... we're snowbirds too, you know."
They both laughed.

"I have a surprise for you. I booked a tour of the winery and wine tasting," he said, taking her hand.

"Oh, good, Josh." She paused. "But we won't forget about Arcadia, right? I had hoped to do some rummaging through the quaint antique shops there."

"There will be time. It's a luncheon tour and then we'll be on our way. I promise." He turned her into his arms and placed a comforting kiss on her lips. "And if you don't get to see them all, we can come back."

They enjoyed the tour and a leisurely lunch of crackers and cheese while sampling the various wines under the vine-covered pergola. Most of the visitors were older couples and groups.

"Is it my imagination or are we the youngest couple there?" she asked looking around.

Josh took her hand in his and gently rubbed his thumb across her knuckles. "Do you know how much I love you?"

Maggie smiled at their joined hands on the table. "Yes, I do. I love you too."

"Well, I was thinking, now that I'm out of law school and starting this great job..." He paused and took a breath. "Well, we might think about a wedding." He pulled a little blue velvet box from his pocket, placed it on the table and very gently pushed it toward her.

"And just whose wedding are you thinking about?" Maggie lowered her eyes and smiled as the picked up the little box. Her voice quivered with excitement.

"Ours! You silly goose," he said, a little louder than he intended. He glanced around quickly to see if anyone had noticed before continuing - a bit quieter this time. "I was thinking about Thanksgiving."

He opened the box revealing a delicate diamond marquise-shaped solitaire.

"Oh, Josh, this is gorgeous."

He took the ring out of the box and placed it on Maggie's finger. The ring sparkled in the afternoon sun flashing tiny specks of light onto the surrounding walls.

"Can we afford it?" she whispered. Sometimes Josh could be very impulsive.

"That's not for you to worry about. I won't tell you the cost; just think of it as an investment."

Her heart leapt. Had she hurt his feelings? Why had she even mentioned it? She felt tears welling and blinked them away. "It's beautiful, and of course I'll marry you."

"Then Thanksgiving is good for you?"

"Next year, right?" she asked, distracted by the emotions she was feeling and by the ring on her finger.

"Well no, this year. That's not a problem, is it?"

"But that's just a few months away. Weddings take time to plan. You have no clue how hard putting a wedding together can be.

"It can't be that tough."

She was thrilled that he wanted to set a date, but November, really?

After lunch they visited the wine shop. Josh chose a Blanc du Bois Classico to go with the stone crab claws he hoped his mom and dad would bring home. Maggie chose the sweeter, Florida Muscadine Blush to go with desert. His parents always treated them to good wine and they were confident they'd chosen well.

The sky had cleared and they'd put the top down again. As Josh drove toward Arcadia they wound past farms and estates and acres of pastures with horses and cattle. The smell of orange blossoms was strong in the air. Occasionally they passed a roadside stand selling oranges, vegetables or plants. They stopped at one called O'Brian's and quickly picked up some strawberries and local honey.

Arcadia turned out to be everything Maggie had expected. The 20 or so shops were all located within three blocks along West Oak Street. Some of the old brick buildings dated back to the early 20th century, making the town feel it had been caught in a time warp. Years ago a fire destroyed most of the old buildings. In rebuilding the town had been careful to keep to the old traditions and now the new blended right in with the old.

They explored shop after shop. Maggie was captivated with the architecture and pointed out various styles as they walked. They stopped in the old Arcadia Opera House, a reconstructed building now converted into a busy antique shop.

Maggie was torn between two items; the first was an oil on canvas by Girard, which measured 31" x 55". Josh reminded her that it probably wouldn't fit in the overhead compartment on the flight home on Sunday. The second, a vintage footed Northwood beaded cable Carnival Glass bowl, the sheen variegated from green to amethyst to aqua to gold.

"This will fit perfectly into a 9" sq box. We'll take it," she said, handing it to the proprietor. Then something else caught her eye; a lovely green Teco pottery vase made in Chicago in the early 20th century.

"Oh, Josh, won't this be perfect for our bedroom?" she gushed. "We'll take this, too."

They took a break and crossed the street to The Shoppe, a quaint ice cream parlor before heading back with their treasures and a few post cards to send home.

"Have you had enough shopping," he asked walking back to the car.

"Actually, my feet ache from all the walking. The next time we go shopping remind me to wear more comfortable shoes. Oh, hasn't this been such a grand day?" She slipped her arm around his. "I love vacations. I love Florida... Oh, and of course I love you, too."

Just then they passed the Rattlers Old West Saloon.

"This place looks fascinating. Dare we stop in?"

Josh could see that she was tired. "It is getting late and we still have the drive back to Sarasota. Maybe we should check it out another time."

"You're right, besides your folks are looking forward to dinner with us. If we leave now we might make it back before dark."

Chapter 4

The sun was setting when they turned west and headed back to Sarasota. Amazing shades of red, violet and flamingo pink spread across the altocumulus cloud formations. Josh pulled the car's visor down to cut the harsh light of the setting sun.

"What? You don't appreciate natures' last hurrah?" she asked, with a laugh.

"I prefer my buttermilk in biscuits."

"Picky, picky. You know, it will all be over in a few minutes."

"I'm all for that," he said, adjusting his head to keep the visor between his line of vision and the horizon.

Maggie laughed and patted his arm. We'll be home soon and I'll pour you a cool one. And cheese! I know you like cheese with your whine."

"Very funny..." he said, squinting, trying to make out the road through the glare of the sun on the windshield.

"I can't wait to show your mom the vase and bowl and then we can all relax on the lanai with a nice glass of Fiorelli's... **Josh, look out!**"

"Oh, shit!" he exclaimed and jerked the wheel a hard left sending them into the oncoming lane. Luckily no cars in sight. He quickly pulled back, pumping the breaks at the same time in an effort to get control as the car fish-tailed across the road. The front tire caught the soft shoulder, propelling them off the road, sheering a sign and sending them nose-first into a deep, water-filled ditch beside the road. The air bags exploded with a deafening bang.

"Oh my god, Maggie! Are you all right?" his hands still gripping the wheel and shaking.

"I, yes... the damn air bag could have broken my nose, but I'm all right."

"What the hell! Was a cow... A COW! - on the goddam highway!" He opened his door and stepped out... and up to his shins in ditch water. "Son of a...!"

The sign they hit had once read: 'Welcome to Edgeville, population 645', but now half of it lay in the weeds, while the other half swung lazily in the slight breeze.

"Josh, Honey, are you okay?

"I'm fine, but I don't think the car is."

Maggie brushed her red hair away from her face and glided awkwardly out from under the collapsed airbag. "Thank God for seat belts and air bags," she murmured to no one in particular and with a sarcastic edge.

"I can't believe this! A damn cow!" he turned toward the front of the car, slipped in the wet grass landing hard on his backside.

"Josh..."

"I'm fine. Wet, shaky and bruised... did I mention pissed!" he said with strong emphasis on the last word.

"Let's call AAA and get some help out here." Maggie pushed on her door, but it wouldn't open all the way. She eased out, barely getting her feet through the opening. She stepped with both feet into the cold, muddy water almost to her knees. "Yuck!"

"We're going to need a tow. I hope we didn't break anything." Josh, surveyed the car, checking for damage, but not being mechanically inclined, he had no idea what he was looking for.

"Maggie, get your phone out. I'll get the rental papers from the glove box. There is probably an emergency number to call."

"My phone? I told you I was leaving mine to charge. You were supposed to bring yours."

"I thought you said leave mine to charge." A look of realization spread over his face. "Great. Here we are, out in the middle of nowhere, stuck in a ditch, no phone and it's getting darker by the minute.

"Oh, Josh, I'm sorry. I should have checked. I had an idea you weren't listening." She perched on the side of the car, the front end stuck in the ditch and the whole thing listing severely to one side. Josh pulled at prickly stickers that clung to his pant legs.

The black cow was approaching. She had meandered off the road, and looking lost, must have decided to join the party. Maggie stretched out her hand and the cow came closer. She sniffed at Maggie's out-stretched hand.

"Don't make friends with that beast! She almost got us killed!"

"She's sorry. Look, you can see it in those big brown eyes."

"You're such a push over," he said moving toward her. He put his arms around her, holding her close and rested his chin on her shoulder.

"I fell for your big brown eyes, didn't I?" She said softly.

"And I'm glad you did." Josh gave her a hug. "It will all be fine. The car is a rental and insured. We'll find a farm house and get some help. I'm sorry, Maggie. I wasn't listening to you about the phone. My mind was on the winery reservations and surprising you."

"You know, most men would be ranting and raving about now. You are always the calm one. I swear you can resolve any problem. That's why you will make one great attorney."

"Oh, I was mad, but there is nothing we can do. Am I going to be mad at the cow? If I'm angry with anyone it's the farmer who let his cow wander all over the road."

"We'd better get going. I saw a house back down the road. Open the trunk, would you? I think I have other pair of shoes in there. I can't walk in these; they're totally ruined."

Josh grabbed their jackets, and Maggie changed her wet shoes. Hand in hand, they walked back the way they had come.

"It's so quite out here - no cars or trucks. Listen, you can hear different insects and a few late birds." Maggie whispered. They could hear the soft sounds of nature settling in for the night. The lights of a farm house shone in the distance, leading the way.

Chapter 5

The moon would not be full for a few more nights but there was enough light to make their way. Before long they came to the driveway leading to the farm house that Maggie had noticed earlier. A handmade sign on the post read: 'Honey for Sale. Come on up.' The sound of their feet crunching on the crushed shell drive resounded in the still night air.

"Sounds friendly," said Maggie. They followed the sign directing them to a parking area behind the house. There were wood steps that led to a large, screened back porch, which extended the full width of the house. Beside the steps a sign read 'Walk In'. They walked up and opened the screen door. They could see that jars of honey had been set out on a table along with bees wax candles in various sizes. A sign listed the prices, and 'Pay Here' was written in huge black letters on a cigar box.

"The owners of this place are very trusting," Maggie whispered.

The farmhouse set back from the road and looked to be quite old, but it was hard to be sure in the dark. Off to one side was a barn, and what appeared to be an orange grove extended back behind the house. The aroma of orange blossoms filling the air confirmed it.

Just then three dogs came racing to meet them, barking and wagging their tails in greeting. The porch light came on and an old woman stepped out. She was short, stout and held a bowl of green beans. She placed it on the floor beside her rocker. "Bella! Blue! Tucker! You get on over here right now and stop scaring these nice folks. Hi there," she said to the couple over the yapping of the dogs. She took a bag of dog food off the table and poured some in each of three bowls of different sizes and then replaced the bag. "I didn't hear a car drive up and now I see why. No car. Did you have a breakdown?"

The old woman spoke with a soft country twang. "Get your nose out of there, Tucker," she said, brushing the black and white collie away from the bowl. "Those aren't for you."

"Well, it wasn't a breakdown exactly. There was this cow in the road and we landed in a ditch." Josh began. Realizing the cow might belong to her, softened his tone. "Uh, we were trying not to hit her, ma'am."

"That's got to be one of ol' Henry Culver's cows," the woman shook her head. "I keep telling that man he's got to fix his fences, but does he listen? No, he doesn't. Somebody's going to sue him for damages one of these days, and then maybe he'll learn - but I doubt it. Come on, have a seat. I'm Mrs. Sullivan. Welcome to Honey Tree Farm."

Josh and Maggie introduced themselves. The age of the woman was hard to determine. She looked to be in her early or mid-eighties. She wore a blue cotton dress that hung below her knees and worn house slippers on her feet. Her hair was a sparkling mix in shades of gray and shined like a halo in the overhead light. Her smile was welcoming and her eyes held a joyful sparkle.

"Thank you, Mrs. Sullivan. Josh said. We're sorry to be a bother, but yours is the first place we came to."

"It's no trouble at all. I'll call down to Barry at the garage. He's got a tow truck and has hauled plenty out of the ditches around here." She went to the door. "I'll get some iced tea for you while you wait. It shouldn't be long. It's a pleasant evening. Have a seat out here on the porch and I'll be right back."

"Mrs. Sullivan," said Josh. "Can I call my folks and let them know what's happened? We were supposed to be back in time for dinner. I should also call the rental company."

"Of course, Josh. I'll call Barry, and then you can make any calls you need to," she answered and leaving the young couple on the porch.

"She seems like a nice lady. I wonder if she's here all alone."

"I'll wager some of these farms have been in the same family for generations," said Josh. "She probably has tons of family nearby to check on her."

Mrs. Sullivan returned carrying a tray with a pitcher of iced tea, four glasses and a plate of cookies. "I got hold of the garage just in time. They were locking up for the night. Barry is out on another call, but they'll get a message to him and have him call."

She set the tray on the table, poured tea into one glass and handed it to Josh. "It's okay if you want to go on in and make your calls. The phone is down the hall and on the right."

Josh wandered inside. A light on the stove lit the room sufficiently to see as he walked through the small kitchen. It looked like an ad right out of a 1950's magazine. There was the white enamel gas stove and a single door Kelvinator refrigerator. The kitchen felt cozy and comfortable. He walked down the hallway and found the phone located on a small table by the stairs. Beside the phone was a little brass lamp with an etched chimney. "That's probably vintage too," Josh said to himself. He almost expected to find an old rotary dial phone, but at least the phone was updated; although, it might have been one of the last phones tethered to the wall.

The handy push-button assembly was on the right side of the cradle in which the receiver laid. The room's decorations and furniture were old and worn, but everything appeared neat and tidy. Family photos were displayed on the wall leading up the stairs probably to the bedrooms. He dialed as he looked them over. Some were quite old. He guessed the newer ones were the woman's children and grandchildren. The phone on the other end began ringing.

Maggie couldn't help admiring Mrs. Sullivan's things as she sipped the cold tea. There was the old rocking chair the woman sat in, the painted tray that held the refreshments and they sat on an ancient wicker table. It had seen better days but still appeared sturdy. This was obviously a woman who took care of her things.

"What a lovely etched pitcher," she said as she took another sip. "I love antiques. It looks to be vintage, but I don't recognize that floral pattern."

"Oh my, I've had that for ages. It used to have matching glasses, but one by one they got broken.

"Would you like a cookie, dear?" She started to get up to retrieve the small plate of cookies from the tray.

"No, let me." Maggie offered the plate to her new acquaintance. "Mrs. Sullivan, isn't it?"

"Yes, but why don't you call me Kathy?"

"These cookies are very good. Did you bake them?

"Oh no, I don't bake cookies or cake." She continued. "I don't bake much at all since the kids grew up. If we need something sweet, the grocery has a good selection. Still, sometimes I get a hankering for something, you know? Just this morning a mood struck me and I made an apple pie for Jesse." She took another sip of tea before she continued. "Jesse, my husband, is very fond of apple pie. I wanted to surprise him with it when he gets home. He must have had a meeting tonight. That's what they call it anyway, but I suspect it's more of a boy's night out in which they share tall tales and local gossip."

Josh came through the screen door and onto the porch. He was met again by the dogs and almost tripped over the little one.

"Shoo," said Katy and waved them away. "Go sit in the corner. Don't be underfoot."

"My folks didn't answer. I'll try again later, but I did leave a message on their answering machine. The rental company didn't answer either. They had a recording telling their hours. Can you believe that?"

"That's the way it is out here. Everything pretty much closes up at night," Mrs. Sullivan said.

"We rented the car at the Tampa Airport. You would think they would have a twenty-four hour emergency number. I guess it will be up to Barry and his tow truck," said Maggie.

"You're probably right. Maybe there is something in the car that I missed." Josh drank the last of his drink. "This tea is fantastic. It's got a different flavor. I don't think I've ever tasted anything like it."

"It's true," said Maggie. "What is that flavor?"

"I put honey in it while it's still warm. There's orange blossom honey in this batch. We like it. Now, tell me what brings you out this way," she asked.

"We were in Arcadia checking out the antique shops." Maggie sat her empty glass on the tray. "We were looking for something for our condo in Atlanta. I found several things to bring home."

"Atlanta, Georgia? You must be on vacation. I did a lot of traveling with my dad when I was young. Never did get to Atlanta though," she replied. "I haven't been to Arcadia in years. We used to go there a lot. They had some fine festivals back then. I remember going to a couple of rodeos out that way with Jesse and the kids when they were little."

"Has your family been on this farm a long time?" asked Josh.

"Well, it belongs to my husband, Jesse. I came here with my father for the first time when I was twelve." Mrs. Sullivan smiled, likely at some long ago memory.

She picked up the blue pottery bowl with fresh green beans and turned them out on the table. She took a handful and began topping and tailing them as she rocked back and forth. The rhythmic squeak, squeak of the chair blended naturally with the nearby orchestra of crickets and frogs.

"Don't you love this time of night? A peaceful quite settles over the farm. You can watch the bats fly in and out of that neglected old barn. She rested her hands on the rim of the cracked blue bowl in her lap, now almost filled with the prepared beans.

Maggie refilled the three glasses and handed Josh his. She offered cookies to the others before taking her chair again.

A little smile danced on Katy's wrinkled face as she remembered a day so long ago. We have time, would you like to hear the story of how I came to be at Honey Tree Farm? I remember that day as if it were yesterday," she said wistfully.

Chapter 6

"They're here! They're here! The bees are here!" Jesse yelled, racing to the kitchen door and out to the farm yard; the screen door banging loudly in his wake. His mother and father came out to greet the visitors followed by three yapping dogs.

A 1942 Chevy pickup turned into the farm yard. Once bright and shiny it was now an old, rusty red flatbed. As it crawled noisily along, a cloud of dust swirled around it. The gears of the truck ground painfully as it slowly came to rest. A big man in jeans and wrinkled plaid shirt hopped down. He took off his battered hat and slapped it against his thigh.

Bees and their honey were his business. He contracted with farmers all across Central Florida for places to keep his hives. He logged a lot of miles traveling from farm to farm placing them and later going back to check on them and collect the honey.

"Hi, folks. Sure hope you are the Sullivans. We got turned around a couple of

39

times. I'm Jim Hailey," he said, shaking
hands with Doris and Ted Sullivan.

Ted introduced his wife and their thirteen
year old son, Jesse, a tall, dark haired boy
with a slim athletic build from working on the
farm.

"If you have a load of bee hives, you have
the right place." Ted grinned eagerly. "I'll
show you where you can place them. The
grove is just out back." He pointed to a couple
of acres of orange trees ready to burst into
bloom.

"It's been a long trip. Mind if my daughter
and I wash up first? It's been a while since we
stopped. These hives have come from a
blueberry farm in Lakeland," said Hailey.

"Sure. No problem. Didn't realize you had
anyone with you. Come on in and have a cold
drink. Then you can tell me all about these
bees of yours," Ted said.

"I'll get Katy." Jim returned to the truck.
He walked to the passenger side and coaxed
his reluctant daughter out of the truck. She
was incredibly shy with strangers, and it took
all her courage to meet new people. She might
have stayed in the truck, but she was
desperate to use the bathroom.

Jesse marched up and jumped on the
running board of the truck next to her. "Hi.
My name is Jesse. Come on, I'll show you
where to go."

Katy turned to look at him. It was something about his eyes that comforted her and when he turned toward the house she fell in step behind him, not unlike a little puppy with a new friend. She was twelve and small for her age; most took her for much younger. Her long hair was the color of summer bleached wheat and plaited in two neat braids. Her pale blue eyes seemed grayer when the light diminished. She wore bib overalls over a pink plaid shirt.

"Well, aren't you the cutest thing?" Doris gushed, following the newcomers into the house. Unused to compliments, Katy blushed crimson and felt the heat in her cheeks.

"Don't mind me, Sweetheart. I hoped at one time to give Jesse a little sister, but it wasn't in the cards." Doris confided. "If you stick around long enough I promise I'll spoil you rotten."

Jim and Katy freshened up. Then Jesse took Katy under his wing while the men unload the bees beside the barn along the perimeter of the orchid. The sun was hot and after several hours of hard work and a few bee stings later, Jim and Ted were ready for a break. The grownups sat in the shade on the porch cooling off with sweet iced tea so cold that the glasses sweat even more than the men. Doris brought out sandwiches and cookies for everyone. The adults chatted about the bee business while Jesse and Katy rested on the steps.

After lunch Jim and Ted went back to work again setting out the remaining hives beside the orange grove. They finished as the shadows grew long.

Jesse and Katy were in the yard playing with the dogs. They were throwing a ball for the dogs to fetch and return. Katy laughed as the dogs tumbled and ran, pushing one another in an effort to get the ball. It seemed like the children had been friends forever.

"Daddy! Daddy, watch Barker. He's the black and white one. He's the fastest. Watch." Katy threw the ball again, laughing as Barker raced the other dogs. "Midge is old and slow, so we throw it closer for her. She's the brown one. Toby likes it high in the air; he can jump really high."

Jim spoke softly. "I am amazed. She has never taken to anyone like she has to your Jesse. She's usually shy, especially with other kids. I'm on the road a lot, so I home school her. She doesn't get to play with other kids her age. She is actually playing like a twelve year old should."

They watched a few more minutes while everyone finished their drinks.

"I wish we didn't have to rush but we have to be on our way. I'll come see you again in a few weeks." He called to the children. "Come on, Katy, it's time to hit the road. Thanks folks."

Katy ran to the truck.

"Say goodbye to Mr. and Mrs. Sullivan, Katy," her father reminded her.

Her head dropped and they barely heard a soft "Thank you for the nice lunch and letting me play with your dogs,"

They watched the truck laboriously make the turn around the yard and grind its way up the drive. Katy turned in her seat and waved to Jesse. He run behind them as far as the entrance to the farm, where he waved until the truck disappeared down the road.

It was three weeks before Jim came back to the Sullivan farm in order to check on the hives. Katy was with him, and in no time she and Jesse were off into the orchard to play while Jim worked with the hives.

"You simply have to stay for supper. It will refresh you for the drive." Jim knew Doris was right, but the aroma of the stew simmering on the stove is what really persuaded him."

Katy was a different person with Jesse and Jim saw it clearly, but what Ted and Doris noticed was the change in Jesse. He played with his other friends, but always checked the calendar on the kitchen wall for when Katy would return.

A few weeks later, the old truck came rumbling up the drive and into the farm yard again. The orange blossoms had finished blooming, and the bees had done their pollinating job.

"Ted," Jim began. "I'm thinking of leaving a few hives here to finish your orange trees. I need to take some over to Plant City. There is a farmer with some sweet clover I'd like to set the bees on."

The men walked down the path toward the grove. "I need to check the hives and the queens. I can make up some splits with the new queens and add some supers to keep your bees from swarming."

"Fine with me," Ted replied. "I've been reading a few books on bee keeping. I was hoping you could leave a couple of hives. I'd like to try my hand, you know, learn to work with them. Jesse seems quite keen to work with them as well."

"Don't great minds think alike?" Jim asked, and the two men laughed together.

Chapter 7

Rousing herself from her reverie Mrs. Sullivan asked, "Would you two like a bite to eat? I have some ham left and could make up a couple of sandwiches. You must be getting hungry, and I haven't had any supper either."

"I'm sure the tow truck will be along soon," Maggie said.

"Well, it will still take him time when he does get here."

"Maybe we'd have just a sandwich, and some more of your delicious iced tea, if you don't mind?" Josh added.

Mrs. Sullivan took her bowl of green beans and the empty pitcher into the kitchen. The dogs followed close at her heels. She put the beans in the refrigerator and took a cold jug of tea out, poured it into the pitcher and added some fresh ice. She turned to the refrigerator and took out the plate of ham. A loaf of bread sat on top and she took that down as well. In a matter of minutes ham sandwiches and pickle spears were piled on two plates. She grabbed the pitcher and carried them out to her guests.

"We didn't mean to make such work for you, Mrs. Sullivan." Josh said, as he took the plates from her.

"I'm just sorry you have to wait like this," she said as she filled and passed the glasses of tea.

Inside the phone rang and Katy hurried to answer it. When she returned she was smiling.

"That was Barry," she said. "He is on the other call, but he'll get to yours as soon as he can.

"We really can't thank you enough," said Josh.

"It is no problem. I love having visitors. One of the reasons I enjoy selling the honey is that we meet some really interesting people, and I like it when it's a family with kids. Our own are grown and busy, although they check in from time to time. Now my grandson, Travis, he comes by a lot. He likes the bees and takes care of them for us.

They shared the ham sandwiches and were savoring another glass of tea.

"May I use your bathroom?" Maggie asked.

"Of course, dear. It's just off the kitchen, to the left. Maggie set her glass down and left.

"Your Maggie has an eye for antiques, I suspect." She said to Josh.

"Oh yes. She was thrilled when she read that Arcadia had so many shops. It's something like 20, I believe."

"Back at the turn of the century - the 20th, not the last one - there was an awful fire. Jesse's parents remembered it. They said it destroyed just about the whole town. How tragic."

"I can't imagine."

"It happened on Thanksgiving day, too. I heard the accident had to do with the phosphate that was mined and shipped from there at the time."

"Any fire is awful, but they didn't have the equipment to put fires out back then like they do now," Josh added.

"A town the size of Arcadia at that time would still be using horse drawn wagons."

Josh chuckled. "Maybe horse drawn wagons weren't so bad. If Maggie and I had been driving one today we wouldn't have had the accident and we'd be home by now."

"I'm not so sure about that. Remember, the pace of life was much slower then. How fast could they go and how far?"

Josh chuckled again. "You're probably right, Mrs. Sullivan."

The sound of the phone ringing interrupted him.

"I'll just see who that is," Mrs. Sullivan said, getting up from the rocker. Carefully dodging the dogs, she left to answer the phone. She passed Maggie at the door.

"You know, I don't mind waiting for the tow truck to get our car out of the ditch," Josh said. "I'm really enjoying her."

"Me too," Maggie replied.

"I do wish we had our cell phones, though. How did people ever get along without them?"

"You can say that again." She grinned, and added, her tone just above a whisper. "This is a little like it must have been back in the old days, maybe the 50s and 60s. She has all these mid-century modern pieces, and this house, and that shell drive. It's right out of American history!"

"Could be," Josh said and laughed too.

The screen door squeaked and Mrs. Sullivan came out the door.

"It's for you Josh," she said. "It's your folks. They got your message and would like to talk with you."

"Thank you, Mrs. Sullivan," said Josh as he rose from his chair.

"We're so sorry to impose on you like this." Maggie was most sincere. "You must have things to do."

"Nonsense, this is a treat for me. I'm just waiting for Jesse to come home. I wish you could meet our grandson Travis. He's a little older than you, I imagine." Mrs. Sullivan took her chair and began rocking again. "Travis loves the bees. He went to college and learned how to take care of them like his grandpa. He's such a good boy. We're going to leave the farm to him one day. We know he'll take good care of it."

The screen door squeaking announced Josh's return. "Dad offered to come get us, but I thought we'd better wait and see what Barry says after he looks at the car. If it isn't too bad, we might be able to drive back to Sarasota. I told him I'd call later and let him know what's happening."

"Don't you worry," Mrs. Sullivan assured them. "Things have a way of working out for the best, even if they don't seem like it at the time. There's no rush, and besides, I like your company."

"Tell us some more of your story, please?" Maggie asked.

Mrs. Sullivan continued rocking as her mind trailed off to a chicken dinner a long time ago.

Chapter 8

Every year at orange blossom time, Jesse
waited for the old truck to come rumbling into
the farm yard, kicking up dust. The truck
would be piled with hives ready to be
unloaded in the grove behind the house.

When he heard the familiar grinding of
gears Jesse ran out to meet them. Katy
jumped down almost before the truck stopped
and ran to give Doris and Ted a hug.

"Hi, Jim," Ted said stepping forward to
shake his hand.

"We've got a couple of nice chickens in the
oven for later," she said as they walked to the
house. "Sure hope you brought your appetite
with you," Doris said. She handed Jim a glass
of lemonade and hugged Katy, smoothing her
golden hair. "I swear you get more grown up
every time I see you. You're almost as tall as
me."

No bib overalls for Katy this year. Her
jeans were gently hugging her teenage curves

and her loose shirt could no longer conceal how she had developed.

Jesse took Katy's hand, pulling her in the direction of the barn.

"I don't know about those two." Jim said. "Whenever they see each other, it's like they have never been apart."

"Should I be worried?" Doris turned to Jim. "Have you had that little talk with Katy?" Doris asked. "You know, the birds and the bees talk."

Jim sputtered, and dribbled tea onto his plaid shirt.

Doris giggled at his reaction and offered him a napkin to wipe his shirt.

Jim blushed. "I... I asked the nurse in the doctor's office to talk to her about that. I just couldn't bring myself to do it."

"Well, I can understand that," Ted said, not meeting Jim's glance.

"The nurse, Mrs. Cotrelle, came to me and asked if I'd given it any thought. Shoot, I never thought much about things like that. It's - you know - girl stuff. I don't know much about that. I have tried to be both mother and father to Katy, but I just couldn't..." His voice trailed off and he cleared his throat.

"I do have some news though," he continued. "It's kind of on that subject. Well, not really. I uh, I've been seeing a lady from Myakka, out near where we live. She runs a little shop and gas station there. We had talked a number of times and I finally got up the nerve to ask her out last summer. I didn't want to jinx it by mentioning it to anyone. Malinda · that's her name · she gets along with Katy real well. I'm thinking of asking her to marry me." Jim took a deep breath, waiting to see what Ted and Doris' reaction would be.

Ted jumped up, bumping the table and splashing the tea.

"Why, you ol' dark horse! You sure can keep a secret," Ted bellowed, reaching out to shake Jim's hand and then he slapped him on the back.

"Oh, Jim, this is wonderful news," exclaimed Doris. "You've been a widower for so long, and it will be great for Katy, too. She will love having another woman around. Have you told Katy your plans?"

"No, but I might soon. I'm just waiting for the right time," he said. "I think I need to work up to it. I think she might be ok with it. She likes Malinda. They go shopping and to movies. They're more like friends really, but I'm keeping my fingers crossed."

"So, tell us more about Malinda," Doris said, "I'm bubbling over with curiosity."

Jim was more than happy to talk about Malinda now that his secret was out, "She's about my age, and Spanish. Her folks came here to work up in Ybor City at the cigar factory years ago. She's a widow with two grown children that live nearby. She's pretty soft spoken most of the time, but her temper can get her going. We joke about that a lot." He grins. "Sometimes I rile her up just to have a bit of fun,"

The adults sat and talked, while the aroma of baking chickens wafted from the kitchen.

Jesse and Katy stood inside the huge double doors. The barn smelled of fresh hay. Jesse had worked all day cleaning out the calves' pen. He had cleaned it for Katy. He didn't want her stepping in cow manure, if he could help it.

"What do you think of the new calves?"

"Oh, Jesse, they are adorable," she exclaimed, looking over the wooden railing into the pen where two sets of dark eyes stared back.

"You can feed them a bottle of milk if you want?" Jesse opened the gate and showed Katy the spot where a clean bale of hay had been put down for them to sit on. He handed her a large bottle of milk and showed her how to hold it up for the calf.

Katy giggled as the small calf nudged her hand and found the bottle. It curled its tongue around the oversized rubber nipple and started to drink. The little cow tugged hard and she had to hold on tight. This made her laugh.

"What are their names?" Katy asked.

"No, we don't usually give them names. They get a tag in their ear with a number on it, but maybe you can give them names," Jesse said. He didn't want to tell her that the calves would be going to market when they got bigger. The profit from raising beef cattle helped to keep the farm running.

Jesse and Katy settled down in the hay. One calf in Katy's lap, the other one in Jesse's while they fed.

"Katy, can I ask you something?" Jesse's tone had turned serious.

"Sure," she said.

"You know I have my driver's license, right? Dad lets me use the truck to go into town. I wanted to ask if you would go to a movie with me tonight. Some friends are going and I'd like them to meet you. I'll understand if you don't want to. We can stay here if you'd rather. We can play a board game or cards, whatever you want." Jesse kept his eyes on the calf he was feeding, too afraid to look at Katy. "I'd like to go, but I want to be with you. Shoot, you're pretty, and smart... and I like you a lot. You're not like those other girls. The ones at school can only talk about clothes and stuff.

"Why, Jesse Sullivan, are you asking me out on a date?" she asked, keeping her eyes on the calf in her lap.

"Well, I guess I am. Would you like to go with me, Katy?" Jesse was blushing and shaking and his hands were sweating. He'd never asked a girl out before. Plenty had wanted him to, but he had never met one he liked enough until Katy.

"I'd like to, Jesse. You have to ask my dad if it's ok. If he says yes, then I'd be pleased to be your date," Katy giggled at the word, and she could feel herself blush. No one had ever asked before, but she didn't want to tell that to Jesse. She suspected that this was new territory for both of them.

The two families sat around the enamel and chrome table with wonderfully smelling food, steam rising from bowls and trays and baskets.

"Lovely supper, Doris." Tom took a chunk of chicken breast and passed the plate on to Jim before reaching for the dumplings.

"Yes, sir. Mighty find supper." Jim helped himself to a chunk of chicken, although he wasn't exactly sure of the cut.

"Jesse, take a biscuit and hand it on, then pass the butter, please," Doris said, reaching to serve herself.

While clearing the table, Jesse asked to be excused and joined the men on the porch.

"What's up with Jesse?" Doris asked.

"Oh, he just wants to talk to my dad about something," answered Katy.

Jesse stood at the door considering his next move. As well as he knew Jim and as often as they had talked comfortably, this was different. He swallowed hard and pushed through the door. He went to stand by Jim and started to speak then forgot what he wanted to say. Jesse was not a shy person, and when he realized he was shuffling his feet, he immediately stopped. He held his head up and began to put his hands in his pockets, then changed his mind. "Mr. Hailey, can I ask you something?

"Of course, Jesse, how can I help? Is this about the bees?"

"Uh, no sir." Jesse cleared his throat. Maybe it would be best to just jump in with both feet. What's the worse he could do? He could say no. But that wouldn't be the worst. What if he laughed? Jesse cleared his throat again.

"What is it, Jesse?"

"Well, you see, some friends and I were thinking of going to a movie tonight, and I'd kind of like... It's a good movie, everyone says so, and I thought maybe, well, I'd like to take Katy. Can she come? It's Saturday night and there's no school tomorrow. But we have to leave pretty soon if we're going to make it before it starts and..." Jesse realized he had suddenly run out of words.

"I don't know, Jesse. We were going to get on the road soon. I have to be up in Brandon early tomorrow morning to pick up a load of hives to move to another farm."

"Jim, you and Katy should stay here overnight." Doris was standing at the screen door wiping her hands on a kitchen towel. She stepped out onto the porch. "You can leave for Brandon from here in the morning. You would have a soft bed and hot breakfast, and then be on your way. It is just a suggestion, but it would save time."

Jesse held his breath and looked from his mom to Mr. Hailey.

"I don't know," Jim began.

There was a moment of silence that felt like eons to the seventeen year old boy standing almost shoulder to shoulder with the girl's father. He saw Jim glance over at Katy. Was he looking for a response from her? She didn't react, but stood waiting.

"Well, if you promise to be careful and come straight home after the movie, all right?"

What had felt to Jesse like slow motion suddenly snapped back into real time. "Oh yes, sir. I promise. Thank you. I'll take real good care of her. I'll drive carefully and have her home on time; I promise." Jesse grabbed Katy's hand and they ran to the house.

"I haven't thought much about Katy growing up and going out on her own; never mind with a boy. It scares me a little, you know, to see my little girl grow up. But, honestly, I'm glad it's Jesse asking.

Doris followed the kids into the house.

"Jesse is washing up," the girl told Doris.

"Come with me. I'll help you get ready." Doris pulled Katy's long flaxen hair up, pinned it in place and added a bow. Then she applied a light shade of lipstick on her lips.

"I've never used make-up on before." She checked her reflection in the mirror atop Doris's dresser and liked what she saw.

"You look great," Doris said. "Let's go down and show you off."

Jesse's eyes lit up when he saw Katy. They said their good-byes and ran to the truck. Jesse opened the passenger door and helped her in. He hurried around to his side.

The parents watched the Ford truck pull out of the farm yard and turn down the drive heading for the road. Then they walked back toward the house.

"I can't say I'm not nervous about Katy being out with Jesse. It's not that she's with Jesse; it's that she's out at all... and with a boy. I suddenly feel very old. My little Katy going with a boy to a movie," Jim said. Taking off his ball cap, he ran a hand through his hair; a habit they knew he employed when he was worried.

"It's getting chilly out here. I'll put coffee on while we wait for them to get back. There might still be some rhubarb pie left in the fridge."

Doris hurried into the kitchen while the two men stood on the porch talking. They could hear her bustling around, opening cabinet doors, drawers, and the refrigerator door.

"Ted, I don't mind telling you this is all new to me. You have to be so careful with a girl."

"She doesn't go out with boys at home?" Ted asked.

"Well, no. I mean she never seemed interested. But, I guess she is growing up. Maybe it's good that I met Malinda when I did."

Just then Doris called, "Come on you two, coffee's hot and pie's ready."

Chapter 9

Jesse pulled the truck into a diagonal parking place in front of the movie house. Several kids were standing near the large poster displayed in a lighted glass front frame. It depicted a pensive blond looking back over her shoulder at a ghostly woman. . Huge white letters spelled out the movie's title: *The Invisible Woman*; the black and white film stared Virginia Bruce and John Barrymore.

The kids all waved and walked over when they saw Jesse get out and open Katy's door.

"Brice insisted on this scary science fiction film. I don't like scary movies. I don't know why we couldn't drive into Myakka City. Maybe the movie there would be better." Janice folded her arms across her chest and silently pouted.

"Hey, what's this? Jesse has a date? And isn't she cute." Brice walked behind her checking her up and down. Katy blushed.

Brice liked being a jock and strutted, rather than walked. At five-foot nine he was

60

shorter than the other two boys. Nonetheless, what he lacked in height he more than made up for in self-confidence. Hank, a burly six feet player on the school football team, was a mountain to be dealt with on the field, but off it he was a tender hearted, gentle giant.

"Just ignore him." Janice told Katy. She took her arm and moved her away from the guys. Cora joined the girls. "He is the quarterback on our football team and he likes to grand stand. I think he's been knocked in the head once too often. My name's Janice and this is Cora. What school do you go to?

"I, uh... I don't go to a school. I study at home," Katy said. She watched their expressions of shock and waited for the teasing to begin.

"Really? Wow! I don't know anybody that studies at home."

"I think it sounds like fun." Cora smiled easily and had friendly eyes.

"The movie is about to start. We'd better go," Jesse called to the others as he took Katy's hand.

"Is this Brice your friend?" Katy whispered to Jesse.

"I don't know him that well. We share a couple classes, but that's all. Hank and I are close friends. We've been pals since kindergarten. I don't know Janice, but she seems pretty nice. She and Cora are cheerleaders.

Katy kept close to Jesse. Once in the theatre he stood back to allow her in the row of seats first and then he followed. Jesse didn't want her to end up sitting next to Brice.

The interior looked very glamorous with velvet drapes and small balconies lining the side walls. Kate observed that the balconies were not real, but they certainly added to the ambiance. The seats were puffy and comfortable and tilted back allowing more room to move past. This movie theatre had four chandeliers; the theatre back home did not.

As the theatre grew dark music began and the *Movietone News* flashed on the screen with the voice of Lowell Thomas. When the movie started a black car pulled to a stop. An elderly man and a woman draped with a scarf over her face - actually, she's covered from head to toe - gets out. The man tells her to go behind them and undress. She says, Oh, let me go like this... and removes the scarf. She has no head! With a gasp, Katy grabs Jesse's arm. Then she chuckled. "Sorry, it just surprised me."

He squeezed her hand reassuringly... and neither let go.

After the movie they walked outside.

"I thought this was supposed to be a scary movie. I thought it was funny," Katy said to Jesse.

"I thought it was about a woman who kept taking off her clothes," Brice grumbled.

"That's exactly what it was," Janice replied.

"You know what I mean."

"Yes, we all do," she said, and the others laughed. "Why don't you have Jesse bring you to one of the football games? You can see us in action and maybe grab a soda with us after," Janice suggested.

"I'd like that," said Katy.

"Let's stop at the ice cream parlor," Brice said. "I'm hungry."

"Sorry, I have got to get Katy home. You guys go. I'll see you in school on Monday.

"Why? Does she have you whipped already? I bet you're just going to go up to the point and get yourself a little." Brice jabbed Hank in the ribs with his elbow.

"Brice, cut that out," Hank said. He was getting annoyed.

"That's it, isn't it? Jesse is getting him some. Why else hang out with a girl like her? I bet she puts out for all her home schooled buddies."

Jesse turned on Brice so quickly he didn't see it coming. He caught him with a right hook on his nose and Brice went down. Jesse stood over him, fists clenched. "Don't you ever say anything like that about Katy!" He turned to her. "Come on, we're leaving."

Katy was stunned. She had never seen anyone get hit before. She had never seen Jesse mad.

Brice was seething. No one had ever stood up to him like that. No one had ever hit him, not even his father; no one.

"Janice, get in the car," Brice barked. It was a liquid, bloody sound. Actually, there had been two sounds: the first was a sound like the breaking of wishbone on Thanksgiving, and the second was the muffled, nasal sound of a person holding his nose as blood dripped down his hand and sleeve. "Those two had better watch their backs. I won't forget this!"

Janice tried to approach him with a hanky to wipe the blood, but he brushed her off.

Cora asked as she and Hank got in their car. "What do you think Brice will do?"

"I don't know. I don't know him well, but from what I've heard, he can be bad news."

"I'm worried about Janice. She's only dated him a couple of times, and I have a bad feeling about Brice.

"Why don't you give her a call when you get home? Make sure she's okay."

Jesse griped the wheel of the truck so tightly his knuckles turned white. He had never been mad enough to hit anyone before. Brice had made him mad and he was also mad at himself.

"Jesse, are you mad at me?" Katy asked.

"I could never be mad at you. Brice had no call to say what he did. I'm sorry you had to hear it," Jesse took a deep breath and tried to relax.

"I don't know what he was talking about, Jesse. It was like he was talking in code or something. I just don't get what it was all about. I guess I'm just stupid," Katy started crying.

Jesse pulled off the road and set the break. He pulled a handkerchief out of his pocket and handed it to her. "It's clean. I didn't use it."

Katy wiped her eyes and gently blew her nose. "I am so sorry."

"It isn't your fault," he began. "Brice is a bully. He was just picking on you because he could."

"I love traveling with my dad, but I guess I missed out on a lot of things other kids know and talk about."

"Katy that is one of the reasons I like you. You are kind and generous, you have a good heart and you don't try to be someone you're not, just to impress people. You are who you are and I like that."

"But I feel so..." she shook her head. "What did Brice say that made you so mad?"

"Brice was saying he thinks the only reason I'm going out with you is for sex."

"Oh, my God! What did I do to make him think that?"

"It's nothing you said or did. You have nothing to be sorry about. Guys like him are all the same. All they want from a girl... and they think every other guy is after the same thing."

"Poor Janice. Is he treating her like that?"

"Janice can handle him. Come here." He put his arm around her and talked softly until he felt her relax against him.

"I'll talk to Cora at school Monday. She'll know. But it's really up to Janice and she'll probably tell me to mind my own business."

"I like those girls," said Katy. "I don't want anything bad to happen to either of them. I would like to have girl friends."

"That is another reason I like you," Jesse said taking her hand. "We'd better go." Jesse started the engine.

They were quiet on the way home, each lost in their own thoughts. But their thoughts were the same. What would it be like?

No one was on the porch when they pulled up. Jesse held the door while Katy got out of the truck. He held her hand all the way to the steps, then stopped. Jesse turned Katy to face him. He drew her closer. She knew he wanted to kiss her. Katy felt a strange sensation in her stomach as he leaned in and kissed her ever so gently on the lips. This was her very first kiss from a boy.

Jesse heard Katy murmur 'Oh, wow' and then hand in hand they entered the house.

Doris and Jim were seated at the kitchen table. Jim walked over and hugged his daughter.

"Did you enjoy the movie?"

"Yes, it was funny," Katy answered. "It was not a scary sci-fi. I don't think that would be my type at all. I like Jesse's friends. Janice and Cora are very nice." Katy avoided telling her father about Brice or the fight with Jesse. He might never let her go out again.

Doris gathered the coffee cups and put them in the sink to wait 'til morning and then they all walked out to the yard

"Maybe you can stay over when you have more time," Doris said. "I'd love to have another girl around once in a while. I'm kind of outnumbered here." She stepped close to Katy and gave her a motherly hug whispering in her ear, "You know, dear, you can always talk to me if you need to. They tell me I'm a very good listener."

Doris watched Jim's truck grind and backfire off the drive and onto the road. Jesse was watching too, hands in his pockets and his mind and body creating images and feelings he'd never had before.

"Time for bed, Jesse. Your dad couldn't keep his eyes open and went up already."

What Doris didn't tell was that she had seen Katy and Jesse kiss on the porch steps.

She wasn't spying. Her chair in the kitchen looked out on the steps. She was thankful Jim was in the opposite chair and didn't see it. She wasn't sure how Jim would react to seeing his daughter kissing her Jesse. Not because it was Jesse. He's probably not ready to see his daughter kissing any boy. She walked down the hall to her bedroom. "Well, how did it go?" Ted asked, as she got into bed.

"Very well, I think".

"There's something you're not telling me," Ted rolled over and leaned on one elbow to look at Doris. "Come on, tell me. You know you're lousy at keeping secrets."

"Jesse kissed Katy," Doris covered her face with her hands. She wanted to laugh. The kiss was so sweet... so innocent.

"Okay," was all he said. Now let's get some sleep, it's late."

They both lay awake thinking. In separate locations miles apart, Jesse and Katy were thinking too; thinking about holding hands in the dark theatre, about sitting close in the truck, and of course the kiss on the steps. These were new feelings and neither were sure what to do with them.

Chapter 10

Jim watched the cream cloud as he stirred his coffee. It swirled around in his cup until it blended into a single caramel color. He could hear Katy moving around in her bedroom. The tiny house near Myakka didn't leave much room for privacy. He was sitting across the table from Malinda and trying to work up the nerve to tell his daughter that he wanted to get married again.

"You know I never did tell Katy about us. Maybe we'll go for a walk and I'll tell her after breakfast."

"I think that's an excellent idea," Malinda said, clapping Jim on the shoulder. "I'm sure she will love the idea. I know she wouldn't deny you the happiness you deserve. She's a bright and loving child."

"You're right. Katy likes you, so maybe she'll like the idea." Jim got up, headed for the stairs and met Katy, who on her way down.

"Oh good. You're up and dressed. I figured you'd be hungry. Melinda is fixing a nice breakfast."

"Care for a cup of coffee? "Malinda called.

"Yes, please," Katy replied.

Katy suspected her father and Melinda were up to something. They were acting strangely all through breakfast. She wondered if it had to do with her. As she took the last piece of toast and spread jam on it Melinda started the dish water and Jim began clearing the table.

"There's no use putting this off," he whispered to Melinda. She didn't respond but smiled at him and winked.

"Katy, how about checking the hives with your old man?"

Katy froze for a moment. What *was* going on? Something was up. Had he found out about the fight or maybe it was about the kiss? She took a deep breath and followed him out the door and down the porch steps.

They walked behind the house to where their own hives were kept. The hives set not far from a bench in the shade of the big oak tree. One sturdy branch of the tree still held the tire swing Katy had played on as a child. She hesitated when he sat down and patted the seat beside him. She sat and waited. Fear crept in and a cold chill came over her. What could she say? What would he do?

"Katy," he began, "you know..." he paused, running his fingers through his hair. Katy took a deep breath and waited.

"Katy," he began again. "You know that I've been seeing a lot of Malinda?"

"Yes?" She answered. Her throat was so dry that it came out like a croak. *What did Malinda have to do with her?* She cleared her throat.

"Well, I want to ask Malinda to marry me, and I need to know how you feel about it."

It was as though the sun cut through the cold and warmed her to the bone. She took a deep, refreshing breath and suddenly couldn't restrain herself. Dad and Melinda! This was about them!

"Dad, I think that's great! No, it's wonderful even." Katy jumped up and hugged her dad around the neck. He was startled by her reaction and let out a moan. "Oh, too tight? Sorry." She took his hand. "That's the very best news ever!"

"Then you're pleased?"

"Pleased! Of course! I had no idea. I... uh, well gosh, now I won't have to worry about you when I'm not around. Oh my gosh." She heard herself stammering and took another breath. "This is so exciting. Can I be a bridesmaid? Can I wear a long dress and maybe flowers in my hair? Would you ask her, please? Please...?"

71

Jim lifted Katy and swirled her around. "You're the best daughter a man could ask for." He beamed from ear to ear. Now all he had to do was ask Malinda, but he already knew she'd say yes.

Katy chattered all the way back to the house and the grin on Jim's face told Malinda that all had gone well.

"Now to make this all formal like," Jim got down on one knee and took Malinda's hand. "My dear, it would make me the happiest man alive if you would marry me... and my daughter."

"Get up, you old fool. Of course I'll marry you."

"Jim took Malinda in his arms and kissed her right in front of his daughter. Then he danced her around the kitchen to music only they could hear.

Katy burst into laughter. It was exciting, if not a little embarrassing.

Melinda motioned for Katy to come join them. "I think I am the lucky one. I get two people to love." She embraced them both tightly and kissed Katy lightly on the head.

A couple of hours passed as Jim tried to focus on various things around the house, but he couldn't contain himself. Now all he wanted to do was to introduce Malinda to the Sullivans. Over the years they had become a part of his life. They would have to come to the wedding. Maybe they'd stand up for them.

Melinda said she was feeling tired and wanted to take a nap.

"I'll take Katy and visit the Sullivans and tell them the news." He kissed her again and she went up the stairs.

Jim and Katy drove straight to the Sullivan farm. They jumped out of the truck, ran to the house. Ted and Doris had heard them pull up.

"Is everything all right?" Tom asked.

Jim took Tom's hand and shook it vigorously and started to hug Doris, but thought better of it. Instead he took a deep breath trying to calm down, but that wasn't going to happen.

"I did it," he said. "I did it! I and Melinda... I mean Melinda and I... you know. I had to speak to Katy first, to be sure it's what she wanted, too. But then I did... and she said yes, and I couldn't wait to tell someone... and of course that had to be the two of you." He caught his breath again. "I would like to bring her out to meet you sometime and of course you're invited to the wedding.

Jesse came running down the stairs carrying his boots and trying to put them on at the same time. He finally gave up and threw them down. "What is it? Is everything all right? I heard you pull up and all the excitement. What's wrong?"

73

"Nothing is wrong. Everything's right! There's going to be a wedding." Jim grabbed his hand and pumped it.

"Jim and his friend Melinda are getting married," Katy said.

"Why don't I fix us drinks and you can tell us all about it," Doris said, and went back inside. Ted slapped Jim on the back as they followed her into the kitchen.

"Married, huh? That's good news. I was afraid it might be something else." he told Katy.

"No, it's all good."

"Oh, good."

Katy started to go in when Jesse took her hand.

"What?"

He pulled her away from the door, took her face gently with both hands and kissed her. It was so good he kissed her again.

"Are you coming?" asked Jim, who was now standing at the screen door.

"Yes, sir," said Jesse and sidestepped Jim as he went into the kitchen. "What just happened?" he said to Katy. "I guess we'll have plenty to talk about on the way home." He was trying to sound annoyed, but a smile played around his lips. It was a good day, and he was a happy man.

Chapter 11

The sound of the phone ringing startled them all.

"I'll see who it is." Mrs. Sullivan got up from the rocker and, dodging the dogs, went to answer it.

"You know I don't mind this waiting, I'm enjoying her story." Josh took another bite of his sandwich.

"Me too," Maggie replied. "I wonder what it was like living back then. No television, no cell phones. No Interstates."

"No condos. The women dressed like *flappers.*"

"No!" she said, with a chuckle. "Flappers were in the twenties. Remember the movie *It's a wonderful life?* That's how they dressed."

"Hey, what do I know? That was something like seventy years ago."

"I love stories like this, where the pace of life was calm and kids played outside, and kissing a boy was thrilling and innocent."

"Do you think kissing me is innocent?"

75

"Well, no. Not you, of course. You're a stud muffin, if ever I knew one."

"Stud muffin! What's that, something like the Pillsbury Dough Boy?"

"No, I didn't mean that." She's laughing now. He gets out of his chair and moves toward her with a menacing look in his eye.

They hear footsteps and he turns just as the screen door squeaks. Mrs. Sullivan is back.

"Oh, let me take those dishes away. I just hate dirty dishes, don't you?" She snatched up the empty plates and silverware and hurried back inside.

"Josh, what are we going to do? What if the tow truck gets the car out but we can't drive it?"

Josh paced. "I've been thinking about that too. The tow truck will bring the car here if we can drive it. If not, he might be able to take us into Bradenton and my folks can pick us up from there. Or we'll get a hotel and worry about things in the morning." He sat down, took Maggie's hand and kissed her wrist. "Things have a way of working out for the best."

"Sometimes you make me so mad," Maggie said withdrawing her hand. "You never worry, and things *do* work out somehow."

Josh smiled. "You worry enough for both of us, sweetheart."

Mrs. Sullivan returned. "Good news. That was Barry. As soon as he can drop off the other car, he'll come get yours. It shouldn't be long now."

"It's getting chilly out here. Would you like to come into the kitchen? We'll leave the pesky dogs outside."

"Mrs. Sullivan, we really appreciate your hospitality," Maggie said, as she picked up the empty tea pitcher and they followed her into the kitchen. Josh brought in the rest of the things left on the table.

"Nonsense," Mrs. Sullivan said. "Having you here is a treat. Maybe Jesse will get back before you have to leave."

"Josh, would you mind bringing the rocker inside?"

"Certainly, Mrs. Sullivan."

Maggie took a seat at the kitchen table.

"Just put it there by the stove," she instructed him when he returned. She reached in a tall free standing metal cupboard cabinet and brought out a basket of yarn, then sat down in the old wooden rocker.

"What have you got there?" Maggie asked, although she thought she knew.

"I've been working on this for months." She pulled out a colorful knitted piece. "It's an afghan for Jesse. I hope to have it finished in time for his birthday. He gets chilled sometimes, even on the warmest nights."

"It's going to be beautiful. Look at those stitches. Where did you learn to do this?"

"I don't know for sure. It seems like I've been knitting all my life. I may have learned from Malinda, but I think I could knit before that."

Maggie thought she saw a wistful look in the old woman's eyes, but then it was gone.

"What happened to Janice? I have a feeling that Brice did something to her."

The sound of knitting needles could be heard as Katy began...

Chapter 12

Jesse went to school on Monday. He didn't
see them in the halls and didn't have a
chance to look for the girls until after History
class. He figured that when he found one the
other was there too. It was in the cafeteria
when he finally saw Cora sitting with Hank.
They were deep in conversation. He hurried
through the lunch line keeping an eye on
them in case they might leave. After paying
at the register he rushed to join them.

"Hey, you two," Jesse said, putting his
tray down and taking the seat beside Hank.
"Have you seen Janice today?"

"She called in sick," said Cora. "I was just
talking to Hank about it. I tried to call over
the weekend, but her mom said she had a
headache. I even went over there, but I was
told Janice didn't want to see anyone.
Something is wrong. I just know it."

Jesse felt something was wrong too, and
he was certain it had to do with the fight with
Brice. Brice had been furious, and from
things he had heard around school he could

be mean. He had to find out if Janice was okay. "I agree with Cora, something has happened. Let's go see her after school."

"How did it go with Katy on the way home?" Cora asked, concerned. "She looked pretty upset."

"Brice scared her with his talk, but we talked, and she's okay now.

"Oh good, I like her a lot, Jess."

"Me, too. Maybe we can go out again sometime, but without Brice!" said Hank.

"Good idea," Jesse said.

Just then Hank got Jesse's attention and nodded at a group of boys standing by the lunchroom door. Brice! Whatever he was saying, made the other boys laugh. He was acting cocky, as usual.

"That's not good," Hank said "He's up to something. Jesse you'd better be careful for the next few days."

"I intend to. I'll see you after school."

The day seemed to drag until the last bell finally rang and school was over for the day. Hank and Cora were outside when Jesse came out. It didn't take long to reach Janice's house. As they approached, they saw her mother coming down the steps.

"Her Mom's leaving. Now's our chance to talk to Janice," Jesse said. "Cora, why don't you go and see if you can get her to open the door."

"Sure, maybe she'll see us if her mother's not around." She walked quickly to the front door and knocked. When she got no response she knocked again. Cora was ready to give up when the front door opened a crack and Janice peeked out.

"What are you doing here?" She asked

Cora could see Janice's face. Her eye was swollen and her lip was split.

"Never mind that," Cora exclaimed. "What happened to you?" Cora waved to Hank and Jesse.

"Please, go away," Janice cried. "I don't want anyone seeing me like this."

"Don't be silly. We're your friends. Now let us in." Cora pushed the door as Jesse and Hank approached.

"Janice, my God, what happened?" Hank asked.

Janice turned away. "Come in and close the door. There's no point telling the whole neighborhood." She went to the couch and curled up. She kept her hand over her eye, but that couldn't hide her embarrassment.

They waited for Janice to speak first, but she only sat there crying. Cora went over, knelt in front of her and took her hand.

"Jan, we're only here to help."

"Please, tell us what happened," Jesse said.

Janice couldn't look at them. "Brice happened to me!" She burst into great uncontrollable sobs.

Hank jumped to his feet. "That son of a ...! He hit you? Did you tell the police? Does your mother know?" It was like an explanation mark to his question when he punched his fist into the palm of his hand.

"Hank's right. You have to report him. He can't get away with this," said Jesse.

"No!" She held her hands out pleading. "And you can't tell anyone either. My mom thinks we had an accident, and that's how I want to leave it."

Cora walked over to them. "Maybe you should wait for me outside. I don't think she'll say anything while you guys are here, but she might talk to me along."

They left reluctantly. Cora sat on the arm of Janice's chair and put her arm around the crying girl.

"Now tell me what happened. It'll make you feel better. I promise not to tell anyone if you don't want me to."

Janice angrily swiped tears from her eyes, took a deep breath and began.

"After Brice and I left, we drove around. He was ranting about how he would get even with Jesse and that girlfriend of his. He drove up at the point near the river and stopped. You know the place. He got out of the car and paced along the shore, kicking at stones. He came back to the car and told me to get out. I was afraid not to do what he said, so I did. We were just walking, not really talking, when he grabbed me. He kissed me really hard. I told him he was hurting me, tried to push him away, but he slapped me and split my lip. I could taste the blood. I tried to run, but he caught me and tore my blouse. He threw me on the ground. He was fumbling with my skirt, trying to get it up. I screamed at him to stop. He told me to shut up that it wasn't anything I haven't done before. I tried to tell him I'm not like that, but he wouldn't stop. I told him I'm still a virgin, but he hit me with his fist. He said he would fix that problem. Oh, Cora, he raped me! He was so rough. It hurt... but he *wanted* to hurt me. When he was finished he told me to stop crying and get in the car. Then he drove me home. He reached over, opened the car door and pushed me out into the street. He said that's what all bitches get, and then he drove away. He left me there, crying in the street.

"I told my mother we had a car crash and I had hit the dash. She was just glad it wasn't worse and that I was alive. Oh, Cora, It was awful. I feel dirty. How could he do something like that?" She wiped her eyes with the palm of her hand. "Please don't tell anyone. I don't want people to know what he did. How could I face the kids at school if they knew?" Her voice rose. "Cora, I can't tell the police. Oh my god, what would he do if he knew I told the police?" The tears came back, but this time it was fear she felt.

"I don't like it that you aren't calling the police and you should at least tell your mother." Cora said. "But I understand and I won't say anything, except...

"No, you must promise!"

"Janice, we have to tell Jesse and Hank."

"No, no, you can't!"

"They have to know. Someone has to keep an eye on Brice and what he's up to. Besides, they're a part of this too. They won't tell anyone, but they have to know."

"How can I ever hold my head up again? Oh, Cora, I'm so ashamed."

"Honey, you didn't do anything wrong."

"But people will think it's my fault."

"The boys won't tell anyone. You get some rest and get better. I have to go, but I'll call you later." Cora said. "And please, call me if you need anything. If you decide to go back to school · you know, when you're ready · Hank and I will walk you to class every day, if we have to."

"I... oh, not tomorrow. That's too soon. Look at me; there would be too many questions. Mom can call and get my assignments. Let's wait and see, maybe next week." She took a deep breath and seemed to relax a little. "Okay, maybe next week. I'll call you. I promise."

Janice walked Cora to the door. They hugged and Cora said, "Please think about telling your mother. She loves you."

Cora told Hank and Jesse about what Brice had done to Janice.

"That creep. We need to do something about Brice!" Hank said. He punched his palm, once, then twice. "That makes me so mad!"

"It makes me mad, too, but we can't do anything right now, and we can't tell anyone. Let's keep an eye on him."

"We should ask around," said Cora. "Let's find out if he's done this to any other girl."

"If I know Brice, he'll be bragging to his buddies. Some of them are on the football team too. I might be able to get some of them to tell me." Hank shook his head. "I just can't believe anyone could be so cruel."

"Be careful, you two. I have to go, but I'll see you tomorrow."

Chapter 13

Outside the dogs began barking and Mrs. Sullivan got up to check.

"What is it?"

They looked back at her and then, as if on command, they raced off into the grove yapping.

"They're after something," the old lady said. "I sure hope it's nothing that will chase back." She chuckled. "One time they chased a skunk into the grove. I bought out all the tomato juice the grocery had to clean the smell off. We tried everything, but those dogs had to sleep in the barn for more than a week.

Maggie walked over to the door and stood by Katy.

"Mrs. Sullivan, I would like to know how you make that ice tea. It isn't a family secret or anything like that, is it?" Maggie asked.

"Heavens no, dear. I'd be happy to show you." She walked over to the sink and Maggie followed. Katy rinsed the pitcher and sat it on the counter and turned on the heat under the tea kittle. From the cupboard she brought down a large glass measuring cup and then opened a canister marked tea. She spooned out several tablespoons of the loose product and dropped it in the measuring cup.

"Oh, you use loose tea?"

"Why, yes. Then I use cheesecloth."

"Cheesecloth? Can you s till buy that?" Maggie asked with a chuckle.

"Oh yes. Would you use anything else?"

"I guess not!" said Maggie, and gave Josh a wink.

"Pour the tea into the cheesecloth, like this," she said. "Give it a twist and knot it. I've been doing it this way for ever so long."

"None of the tea falls out?"

"No." She dropped the cloth of tea into a saucepan and reached for the tea kittle. "Pour about 3 cups... I don't usually measure any more, but this is how you would want to do it when you begin. About 3 cups of water over the bag of tea and put it on the stove to boil. Boil it about a minute, than let it steep for about 10-12 minutes."

"Oh, isn't this exciting, Josh!" she said turning back to him. "This is how we'll make *real* iced tea from now on."

"While the tea is steeping we get the honey." From the cabinet Katy brought out a big crock with a tight fitting lid. "You don't refrigerate honey, you know. That would change the color and most certainly the flavor. When the time is up we'll remove the tea bag and add a half cup of honey to the water."

"That doesn't seem like enough tea." Maggie said looking into the saucepan.

"Oh, but we aren't finished yet."

"I can't wait to make this for Josh's parents," Maggie said. "They will love it."

From the refrigerator Katy filled the measuring cup with ice and poured it into the pitcher. "Now I pour the tea over the ice, and fill the pitcher - this one is a gallon size - with cold water.

Just then there was a scratching at the door. That is probably Bella. Josh, would you let her in?"

Josh opened the door and the small dog ran immediately to Katy. She gave a long handled spoon to Maggie.

"Why don't you stir it, dear. Once it's cool it is ready to drink."

"That's all there is to it?"

"That's all." Katy picked up the little dog and carried her to the rocker. "Did those big boys fun off and leave you behind? Those bad boys," she cooed as she took her seat. Before long the small dog was asleep in her lap. "This is Bella. Someone just dropped her off by the road one day. Bella is a sweetheart." She stroked the dog's fur. "We're so happy her owners left her with us."

"Mrs. Sullivan," Maggie asked. "What happened to Janice and Brice? I'm afraid

Barry might come to tow our car before you get to finish your story."

"Well, we can't let that happen, can we?" she said, with a smile.

Chapter 14

Back in school the next day, Cora, Hank
and Jesse ate lunch together, which they did
most the time. Brice was eating at another
table with his friends. He would look their
way, nod to his friends, say something and
they would all laugh.

"The guys are giving me a hard time,
Jesse," Hank said. "They're saying that
football practice is going to get pretty rough if
I keep hanging out with you."

"Brice is stirring them up, Hank. I don't
want them hurt you," Cora said, rubbing his
shoulder reassuringly.

"Aw, I can take a couple of tackles.
Besides, this full back can tackle right back,
and they know it."

"Did you talk to Janice this morning?"
Jesse asked.

"I got her mother on the phone. I told her
I'd heard about the accident. She said that
Janice would be out of school the rest of the
week. When I asked to speak with Janice, she
said she was still sleeping. I got the feeling

90

she was hiding something. I wonder if Janice told her what really happened. In any case, she should see a doctor."

Hank, elbows on the table, watching Brice between bites of his sandwich. "What do you mean, just in case?"

"Hank, you can be incredibly dense sometimes," Cora said. "You know, in case she's pregnant."

"Oh man," Hank said. "I didn't think of that. Janice must be going crazy with worry."

"That's why she should tell her mother," Jesse confirmed. "She's going to need her."

Janice came back to school the following week. Her eye was still tender but her Mother helped her cover it with make-up. Then, of course, they all worried together. They stayed away from Brice, but they could see him and his pals watching and whispering in the halls.

A couple of days later, Janice was all smiles and pulled Cora off to the side. She whispered something in Cora's ear, and both girls got excited.

"Oh, thank God," Cora said and hugged her friend fiercely. Tears ran down both faces. This disaster had been averted. Brice watched the exchange and knew he was safe, at least for now.

The following Saturday Jim and Katy stopped by the Sullivan farm on their way home. Doris set out a nice lunch on the porch for all of them.

"Katy, pass your father another chicken salad sandwich, and if anyone wants pickles, you'd better speak up before my son eats them all."

Jesse looked up in surprise. His expression made everyone laugh. It wasn't until then that he realized his mom was teasing.

"Here," Ted said. "Have some more iced tea."

"We have lemonade, too," added Doris.

"What's for desert?" Jesse asked.

"I helped your mother make the strawberry shortcake," Katy replied, proudly.

"After lunch I'm going to take Katy to see how the calves have grown," Jesse announced.

"Jesse said no one named them so I came up with a couple of names. Would that be okay, Mr. Sullivan?" Katy asked.

Ted looked from Doris to Jim. "Well," he began slowly choosing his words carefully. We don't want to get too attached to them. They will be leaving us in a while."

"I won't get attached," she said. "I just think they should have names. Would that be all right?"

Ted looked at Jim for support.

"As long as you understand that they won't be around for long. *Do* you understand?"

"Yes. I do."

"Then it's all right with me." Jim said and took another bite of his sandwich.

"Well, all right is all right," Ted said, settling the whole issue.

"Do you want to know their names?"

"Of course, we do. What names have you chosen?" Doris seemed truly interested.

Katy sat back in her chair and made her big announcement. "I thought about it a lot. I have picked the names..." she paused, looking at each one; ready for their reaction..."Roy and Dale!"

The others glanced around. It was like someone told a joke and no one got it.

"Don't you understand? Roy and Dale **Evans**. They are a cow-*boy* and a cow-*girl*."

Everyone burst into laughter.

After lunch Jesse and Katy strolled to the barn to check on Roy and Dale. Jesse explained how starting tomorrow they would spend their days outside in the pasture and come back into the barn at night. In time they would remain with the rest of the cattle all the time.

Jesse showed her how to spread more straw. They were too big to be bottle fed now, so she took handfuls of grain and they ate from her hand.

"Katy, I have to tell you something. I promised I wouldn't tell anyone, but I have to

tell you. It's about Brice. He's not only ugly
and crude, he's very mean. That night you
met him... after we left, he beat Janice up
and... Well, he hurt her really bad."

"Oh my. Is she all right?" Katy was
stunned. He beat her up? Why?"

"Brice is a bad person. He's mean. He says
and does things to hurt people. Like what he
said about you. He'd never met you before. He
didn't know you. He just said it to be mean."

"But, Jesse. What can we do?"

"We can't do anything about it now," Jesse
said. "Hank, Cora and I are watching him. We
are avoiding him and don't want to cause
anymore trouble. But he knows we're on to
him. It's only a matter of time before he slips
up and gets caught."

Katy leaned her head on his shoulder,
"Can he hurt you? I don't want anything to
happen to you."

"I'm being careful, but if it comes to a
fight, I won't back away." He held her close.
"Don't worry. Nothing's going to happen."

They were quiet for a moment enjoying
the various smells of the barn: the hay and
grain, the two young calves nearby and the
warmth of one another.

Jesse broke the silence. "Oh, I want to
show you something." He rose, took her hand
and led her to the wooden ladder nearby. He
started up first. "Climb up here. You're going
to like this." She followed him up to the loft

94

where more hay was stored. He put a finger to his lips signaling silence and motioned for her to follow. He led her to a dark corner of the loft and pointed at something in the straw. She peaked in and saw two eggs almost hidden from sight.

"Oh, what are they?" she whispered.

"They're barn owl eggs. I saw the mother fly out one morning and I found these."

"When will they hatch?"

"I don't know, but I'll keep watching."

They climbed back down the ladder. At the bottom Jesse took her hand and helped her the rest of the way.

"I have something to ask you."

"Does it have anything to do with Barn Owls or cows?"

"No," he said rolling his eyes.

"Does it have anything to do with movies?"

"No," he repeated. It has to do with the prom that is coming up at our school in May. I want to ask you if you will go to the prom with me."

"Hm." She put her finger to her chin as if thinking. "Let me check my calendar. I have such a busy schedule."

Jesse's smile fell away. "Really?"

"No, silly. I am just kidding," and she tickled him in the ribs and ran out the barn door.

"Oh, okay," just getting the joke, he ran after her. They ran into the grove and past the bee hives. The day was unseasonably warm with few clouds in the sky. He was almost out of breath when he caught her.

"So, what is your answer?"

"First you have to answer a question I have."

"Okay, what?"

"What's a prom?"

Jim stood on the screened porch and called, "Come on, Katy girl. We have to get going. Malinda is waiting for us. That got Katy moving. The two ran back to the house.

"We're coming, Dad," she called as they reached the barn yard. "I got to go," she told Jesse, and without warning she kissed him on the cheek. "See ya."

"Oh boy," Jim said as he watched from the porch. He lifted up his hat and combed his fingers through his hair. "I sure wish she was a boy," he mumbled. Doris smiled.

The gears whined as they pulled into Malinda's crushed shell driveway. Katy was out and running to the front door before Jim even turned the engine off.

"Hi, Malinda," she called.

Malinda came out of the kitchen, a potato masher in her hand, "Hello. You look all shinny and excited. What's going on?"

"Oh, Malinda. I am so happy. Everything at the Sullivan farm makes me happy. The calves are growing like crazy, the bees are buzzing, and Jesse found owl eggs in the loft. What could be more wonderful in the world?"

Melinda smiled and returned to the kitchen. "I understand what makes things so wonderful in the world."

Jim came into the kitchen carrying some rags and an oil can. "I'll be in back. I'm going to see what I can do to fix that old rattle-trap."

"My guess is it needs to be planted. That old truck died ages ago and you never bothered to bury it."

"Very funny," he said, and kissed her on the cheek. "I'll be in the back trying to raise her from the dead."

Jim walked out whistling softly. Katy, who had headed for her room could be heard humming to herself. Melinda sighed. "Oh yes," she said. "I *do* understand what makes things so wonderful in the world."

The pleasant atmosphere still hung over the house when they sat down at dinnertime.

Jim reached for the bowl of mashed potatoes, but Melinda rapped his hand and made a Spanish sound in her throat. "We'll give thanks first."

He quickly withdraw the hand and bowed his head as Melinda made the sign of the cross.

"Bless us, oh Lord, for these thy gifts, which we are about to receive, from thy bounty through Christ, our Lord."

They all responded, "Amen."

Jim reached for the bowl of potatoes, hesitated and glanced at Melinda. She smiled at him under her eyelashes, helped herself to one of the pork chops and handed the platter to Katy.

"How did it go with the funeral?" Melinda asked.

"Not much change, I'm afraid. I should take it to the shop and let them look at it, but I hate to spend money for something I can do myself."

"I guess it's that or you better buy a shovel." She helped herself to the salad and spooned the homemade dressing over it.

Katy sat looking from one to the other trying to figure what they were talking about.

"Did someone die?"

"Some *thing*. Yes." Malinda said.

"No." Jim said.

"Is this an argument?" Katy asked, and rubbed the back of her neck.

"No," said Jim.

"Maybe," said Malinda.

Katy just shook her head and took a mouthful of green beans.

"I have been thinking." Jim put down his fork.

"Of getting rid of it?" Malinda asked.

"No, miss smarty. I think we should set a date to get married."

This got Katy's attention.

"I've been thinking about that, too," Malinda said. "Why don't we plan it for right after Easter? The weather is usually good then, not too hot, and the rains haven't started."

"That sounds good. Where did you have in mind? I was thinking about the Bethany Baptist Church. It's a quaint old church."

"My family is Catholic." She wiped her mouth with her napkin and took a sip of her lemonade. "There is that new church in North Port Charlotte, St Anthony of Padua. It would be a new church for a new family." She paused, thinking. "The grounds are lovely with several old oak trees. I can call tomorrow and talk to the priest. What do you say?"

"I like that," he said, still chewing.

Katy is following this conversation with interest.

"We'll have to register and announce the bans, but there is time for that." She took another sip.

"We don't want anything too fancy, do we? Just us and a few friends would be nice." Jim added.

"Can I invite Jesse, Dad?" Katy asked.

"Of course. I already talked to the Sullivans about it. I've always planned on

asking them, and they'd like to meet you,
Melinda."

"We should do that soon. Do you want to
invite them to your house, or shall we ask
them here?"

"You decide," he said, and forked another
pork chop.

"Dad, we should probably begin making
plans. Malinda will need a new dress and
shoes. We should have flowers. Dad, you
should make a list of all your friends, and
Malinda, too. We'll have to send invitations.
That's how it's done, you know."

Jim and Malinda grinned at each other.

"You're right, Katy. We have to remember
how it's done, and do it right."

"But we don't want a big wedding... just us
and a few friends, right?"

"Oh... okay, Daddy. After all, it is your
wedding too." Katy's expression and manner
reminded him of old Mrs. Roth, his high
school teacher when she was *practicing
patience.* "Maybe I should make a list."

"That would be nice, dear." Malinda said
hiding a smile behind her napkin. What a
change from that shy little girl she had met
not so long ago?

Chapter 15

Mrs. Sullivan stopped to change colors in the afghan. "Don't you think this is a lovely shade of blue? Blue is Jesse's favorite color."

"It is a lovely shade. I'm sure he'll like it," Maggie said. "My favorite is yellow," she thinks for a second. "Josh, I forget. What is your favorite color?"

"I thought you knew. It's green."

"It's funny, I can remember things so clearly from seventy years ago, but sometimes I can't remember whether or not I swept the porch!"

Maggie smiled. "Josh forgot to bring his cell phone and that was only a few hours ago."

"Now, let's be fair. I didn't forget. I misunderstood. There is a big difference. Besides, I wasn't thinking about cell phones. I had more important things on my mind at the time. Show her," he said, nodding to Katy.

"He wants me to show you this," she said and held out her hand to show off the ring.

"That's very pretty. I'm so happy for the two of you. When is the big day?"

"Around Thanksgiving..." Josh began.

"Thanksgiving, next year." Maggie corrected.

"Oh, it's still in the planning stage, is it?"

"Maggie thinks it will take a long time to arrange. But Jim and Malinda did it in a matter of weeks." He sat back in his chair and smiled at Maggie, as if he had just proved a point.

Chapter 16

Katy and Malinda had just finished washing the luncheon dishes when Katy asked. "When can we go shopping?"

"That's a good question. I can order something out of the Sears catalogue, but it might not get here in time. Sometimes the mail is very slow. Or I could have something altered, but I don't think I have anything that would work."

"But, Malinda. You have to have a new dress!"

"Since I was married before, I don't need a big white wedding. But you're right, a new dress would be nice."

"Of course! It's tradition! You have to have 'something new' and that means a new dress."

"I should, and I don't want to leave everything to the last minute either." Malinda thought a minute. "Go get the phone book and we'll pick out a couple dress shops. Why don't we plan to go next weekend? If I can't find anything, we can always reconsider the Sears catalog. We'll have a girl's day out

103

with shopping and lunch. How does that sound?"

"Perfect. I'll get the phone books."

Malinda hung up the dish towels to dry as Katy came back with the books. They laid it out on the table and turned to the yellow pages.

The next Saturday Katy and Malinda got ready to go shopping. Both wore a simple dress, comfortable shoes, white gloves, and of course their purses. They got in Melanie's car and took off for Bradenton. The shops they had chosen were on Manatee Avenue. Both were looking forward to a fun filled day together.

"Malinda, can I ask you a question? Do you know what a prom is?"

"Of course."

"Well, Jesse asked me to go with him to a prom in May."

"A prom? How wonderful! You've never been to one?"

"No. Have you?"

"Oh, I've been to a few proms in my day."

"A few! Wow, you must know all about them."

"I suspect I do."

Malinda saw a sign that read 'Bradenton' and an arrow pointing right. She made a hand signal and turned.

"A prom is a dance, usually held during the senior year of school. All the kids dress up and the boys buy the girls corsages. It's not as important as a wedding, but it's very important to graduating seniors.

"It sounds like fun. I'll bet Hank and Cora will be going too. I'll ask Jesse, maybe we can all go together."

They parked the car on the street and headed for the first shop on the list. The showroom windows on either side of the door were filled with mannequins dressed in the latest fashions.

"This shop looks very nice," Katy said, as she studied the assortment.

"It looks very expensive," said Malinda, as she pulled Katy through the door. They stood for minute and looked around studying the layout. They went through the dozens of dresses hanging in alcoves on both sides of the store. A platform in the center of the store displayed two mannequins standing back to back and the whole thing revolved slowly. One section held fur coats and capes. Another section held formalwear and various lighted cabinets displayed jewelry and handbags.

A blond salesclerk approached. "May I help you, Madam?" she asked.

Katy thought she must have a cold or a stuffy nose from the tone of her voice.

"We're looking for a wedding dress," Katy
replied with a smile.

The woman's neck must have hurt too, for
she didn't move her head but simply looked
down her nose at the Crackers from Myakka.

Malinda was short and curvy and the
things in the shop seemed more for tall and
willowy women.

Finding nothing appropriate, they left.
Once out on the street Malinda said, "I guess
we two poor county mice will just have to take
our business elsewhere."

That struck Katy funny and both women
laughed heartily.

They walked to the next stop just a block
or so away. It too had items displayed in their
showroom windows. They entered and were
greeted by a pleasant saleslady. She asked
their names and introduced herself as Mrs.
Waverly. She asked questions about the
wedding and made suggestions about styles
and possible colors.

"What about an ivory or pastel, Malinda? I
have a lovely ivory ballet length dress. Let me
pull it out for you."

"What's ballet length?" Katy whispered.

"I don't know, but we're about to find out."

Mrs. Waverly came back and showed
Malinda into a dressing room. "You really
have to try it on to appreciate the styling. It is
taffeta with a full skirt and a cute bolero
jacket." As she talked she hung several items

on the hook in the room. "The detailing around the jacket is repeated on the front of the dress; very elegant and not over stated." The saleslady proceeded to help Malinda into the dress.

Mrs. Waverly zipped the dress up and turned Malinda to face the full-length mirror.

"Oh my, this is perfect, but how much?" Malinda asked, twisting to get a better view of all sides.

"This was made for another customer, but she didn't come back for it, and we can't reach her. Since she already paid a deposit, you can have it for the balance."

"It fits you perfectly." Katy said.

"Even the length falls right where it should. It's like the dress was intended for you all along."

"Oh my. This dress just what you need!" Katy was overjoyed.

"I have a hat with a small veil that will go perfectly with the dress, and we can dye shoes to match. Your daughter is right. It's perfect for you."

Malinda liked the sound of that. She would soon have a daughter!

While Malinda changed out of the clothes Katy scanned other racks. She was checking sizes and prices. What a huge selection of colors. How could anybody choose just one?

"Dad's going to love it," Katy said as she joined the women at the cash register.

"That's settled then, I'll take it and the hat. How soon will the shoes be ready?"

They finished the purchase. Malinda swallowed hard when she read the total and reached in her purse to pay. Still, considering it is the perfect dress and accessories, she decided she had done very well.

They left the store feeling jubilant.

"That was exciting," said Katy. "Maybe we can do it again when I go to the prom."

"That is a good idea. We'll do that." Malinda took a deep breath. "Let's get some lunch and relax before we head back? I saw a little café with outdoor seating in the next block."

Malinda opened the trunk and put her purchases inside. They got in the car, pulled away from the curb and headed along Manatee Avenue."

The cafe was shaded by several Pin Oak trees that lined the block. Tables were set for lunch and the two women sat down and placed their orders.

"I'd like some iced tea and a hamburger sandwich, please." Katy took off her gloves and spread her napkin in her lap.

"I think I'll have a chicken salad sandwich and a glass of lemonade," Malinda added. They had just finished their lunch and the waiter brought back the change from the bill when Malinda saw Katy grow pale and stared at a car pulling in.

A cream color 1947 Ford coupe convertible pulled up to the curb.

"Katy, are you all right? What's wrong?" She gripped the girl's hand.

"I know that car. That's Brice. He was with Janice when we went to the movie."

Katy was shaking, but the driver of the car just sat there, watching.

"Come on, let's go."

Malinda was gathering her gloves and purse to leave when Brice opened the car door and got out. He slamming the door so hard several people looked his way. He hopped a low decorative fence around the tables and was at Katy's side in an instant.

"Well, well, if it isn't Miss Goody Two Shoes," Brice snarled.

"What do you want, Brice?" asked Katy quietly, pulling on her gloves and picking up her purse.

"I want you and that boyfriend of yours to keep out of my business. I know you've been asking around about me. What I do is none of your business. That Janice bitch had it coming to her." Brice's voice was carrying and others turned to listen.

"No one deserved to be beaten and raped!" Katy was angry and shouted.

"You keep your mouth shut," he said in a lower voice. "You and your friends better watch it! And you, you'll get what all bitches get."

Suddenly a pitcher of ice water was dumped over Brice's head. The ice ran down his face, soaking his shirt and leaving him sputtering.

Katy grabbed the pitcher from Malinda and put it on the table. Then they jumped in the car and started the engine.

"I'll get you, you bitch, and Jesse too. You'll pay!" Brice was screaming, but his voice faded as they sped away. Katy turned to see him kick the little fence around the tables. The waiter came out and began yelling at Brice.

Katy was shaking from the adrenalin rush, but she burst out laughing. Malinda looked at her in surprise.

"Katy, he's dangerous. I think we should call the police," said Malinda, her own hands shaking on the wheel.

"No, please, that will only make things worse," Katy was still shaking. "Oh, my gosh, that scared me to death." Another burst of laughter. "I'm sorry, Malinda, but you should have seen the look on his face when you hit him with that ice water!"

"I can't believe I did that," she chuckled, "but he made me so mad."

"Jesse had better behave himself with *you* around," Malinda quipped. They both laughed harder and the tension began to ease.

Malinda took the long way home, avoiding the main roads. "Ok, can you tell me what that was all about?" Malinda asked, but watching the rear view mirror just in case.

"Brice was Janice's date when we went to the movie that time, remember?"

"I remember. So why is he so mad at you and Jesse, and what's this about someone getting raped?"

"Something happened that night," Katy said. She took a deep breath and proceeded to tell Malinda how Brice had made fun of her all evening. She told her what he had said about her and Jesse.

"I swear we've never done anything like that. We kissed a couple time, nothing more." Katy confessed.

"Jesse got so mad he hit Brice and knocked him down. Brice was furious. On their way home Brice went off on Janice. Jesse told me she wouldn't go to school after that. She had a split lip, a black eye and she admitted Brice had raped her. She wouldn't go to the police. Brice really hurt her."

"My goodness, honey, how could you keep all this inside?"

"Cora has been asking the girls at school about Brice. She's trying to find out if he's done this before. If other girls will stand up, the police will have to do something about him. He thinks because his father owns Bachlund Motors that he is a big deal around here and nobody will touch him."

"We have to tell your dad about this, and Jesse's parents too," Malinda counseled.

"I was afraid to," Katy said. "I thought Dad might not let me see Jesse again."

"Katy, this is not Jesse's fault or yours.

"Malinda, we just can't tell dad. He will get mad and aggravate the situation. Jesse and Hank want to get more information so when we can go to the police they will have to listen. Please, promise me you won't say anything."

"Katy, how can I begin a marriage with a secret? He might never forgive me."

"Please, once we have what we need we'll tell him. Dad is big on promises. If you promise me, he will not fault for keeping it."

"I hope this can be resolved soon."

The rest of the ride home was quiet, each lost in her own thoughts.

The next day Jim took Malinda to meet the Sullivans. Ted and Doris were so pleased to finally get to meet her.

"I brought you this. It's the first invitation to the wedding. Katy has a list of things we must do beforehand and invitations are high on the list." She handed the small envelope to Doris.

"It's beautiful. Did you draw this?"

"I dabble in art. My shop is full of cards and small landscapes that I've painted and I carry some art supplies. We're only inviting about 20 people; family and friends. We wanted you to be the first."

Doris smiled and patted her hand.

"Your family has been so kind to Jim and Katy."

"Over the years we've become good friends. We are looking forward to the wedding. If there's anything you need, just ask,"

"Well... Jim and I were wondering if the two of you would stand up with us."

Doris' eyes light up and she looked over at Tom. "I would love to!" Doris replied. "It is so sweet of you to ask. Ted, what do you say?"

"We'd be happy to," he said matter of factly.

"Would that include helping with the arrangements?" Doris asked, turning her full attention to Malinda.

"Oh, yes. I figure you, Katy and I can sharing ideas will make the planning all the more fun."

"I want to hear all about your dress."

"Jim, I believe that's our signal to get out of here and let the ladies talk. Let me show you the hives. I've been doing some work with them and I'd appreciate your advice." Ted held the door and Jim went down the steps.

Well, you have to make sure they stay healthy. Did you check for mites? Those pesky critters can cause havoc in a hive." The men walked toward the orange grove.

Katy and Jesse talked as they approached the pasture where the calves were cavorting in the field. Leaning on the fence, they watched Roy and Dale, now almost as big as the other cows.

They stood quiet a moment then Katy spoke. "Running into Brice at the café was awful. You wouldn't believe how he talked, and in front of Malinda too. But she's no fraidy-cat. She dumped that pitcher of water right on his head.

Jesse put his arm around her shoulders. "I'm sure it was very embarrassing.

"I was having such a good day with Malinda, and he ruined it," Katy put her head on Jesse's shoulder. "I'm afraid he's going to do something terrible. Jesse, I don't understand why he's like that."

"Brice is a bully," said Jesse. "When I stood up to him and wouldn't let him get away with the way he was talking about you, he couldn't deal with it. He has to prove he's the big man. He gets away with everything. His mother left them when he was a kid and I think that hurt him more than he'll admit. His dad's busy making money and has no time for him. He gives him new cars anytime he wants. I think his dad hands him money to keep him out of his hair."

"I feel sorry for him. My mom died when I was little, but my dad took me everywhere. He home-schooled me and taught me

114

everything I know. He shows me how much he loves me every day."

"Brice wasn't so lucky, and I think he's jealous of you."

Katy stepped away and looked at Jesse. "Jealous of me? How can he be jealous of me? I'm just a bee keeper's daughter. He's the son of one of the richest men in the county."

Taking her shoulders, he said, "He is jealous because you're sweet and kind and most of all loved." Jesse stepped closer and kissed her lips. "Mm, that's why he's mad; I found you first. We'd better go back." Jesse took her hand.

"I talked to Cora after I talked to you and told her about Brice. She said almost the same thing." Katy stopped suddenly, "Hey, I almost forgot. The prom. Do you still want me to go?"

"Yeah." He stopped dead in his tracks.

"Good. Can we go with Cora and Hank?

"Yeah."

"Can you say anything besides yeah?"

"Well, yeah!" They both laughed. It will be held in the school gym and kids will decorate it. This year the theme is Venice, Italy. It's May 28th, just before graduation. There will be a band and refreshments."

"Oh, Jesse. It sounds like such fun. I'm so glad you asked me."

"Yeah?"

"Yeah. And don't start that again." They both laugh. Jesse leaned over and kissed her cheek.

"I really enjoyed shopping with Malinda for her wedding dress. That was so much fun until..." she shook her head. "I don't want to talk about *him* anymore. I won't rent space in my head for him!" She closed her eyes and took a breath. "Malinda said we would go sometime to look for a prom dress. I'm really looking forward to that." She took his hand and they walked back to the house.

Malinda and Doris were in the kitchen discussing what food would be nice for the wedding reception. "I am so happy you agreed to be my matron of honor. The three of us will make a good team."

"You mean you, me and Jim?"

"No, you, me and Katy. Jim wouldn't be much help, he just agrees to everything."

"You picked the date, I see."

"I called the church and the priest was most helpful. May 8, is open and that will give us time to do everything. We can have the reception in the church basement."

"Malinda, is that what you want?"

"Actually, Jim and I would both prefer to have it at home. It would be more comfortable then in some big open room."

"Your house or his?"

"I think mine. But we will live in his."

Jesse and Katy were sitting on the steps, playing with the dogs when the men returned.

"I'm so happy we finally met. I'll pull out some of my favorite recipes for you to look over," Doris said and gave her a hug.

"Ted, that'll work. You'll see."

"I would never have thought that powdered sugar would do the trick. Thanks, Jim."

Malinda opened the screen door and stepped between Jesse and Katy on the steps.

"Come on, Katy. Time to go," said Jim.

"Good-bye, Mr. and Mrs. Sullivan," Katy said, standing up. Jesse walked her to Malinda's car. He opened the passenger door for Malinda, who got in first, and Katy sat in the back. Before he closed the door he leaned in and gave her a quick kiss. They all waved till the car turned toward Myakka.

"Should I be asking what your intentions are toward Katy, Jess?" Ted asked his son.

"Dad, I'm not sure, but I'm going to figure it out."

"I think you already have and don't know it yet," Ted laughed, putting his arm around Jesse as they walked back to the house.

Chapter 17

"Biscuits, oh my, that does sound good," said Mrs. Sullivan." She was looking at something off in the distance. "I think I'll whip up a batch tomorrow for Jessie. I'll bake a nice chicken and hot biscuits would be perfect."

Josh and Maggie looked at each other wondering what had made the woman think of biscuits in the middle of her story.

Just then the Bella began barking. She jumped from Katy's lap and ran to the door. Outside the other two were frantic and barking. It was obvious someone was approaching.

A handsome young man knocked loudly and walked into the kitchen, the dogs followed yelping and jumping. The stranger was tall and dark and wrinkles were just beginning to form at the corners of his eyes. He wore a weathered cowboy hat that sat at a jaunty angle.

"Hi, Gram. I was driving past and saw the lights on. I see you have company,"

Josh stood up and shook his hand. "I'm Josh Beaumont, and this is my fiancée Maggie. A cow forced us off the road and into a ditch. We ended up here waiting for a tow truck. Mrs. Sullivan has been entertaining us while we wait."

"It's good to meet you. I'm Travis," he said. "That friendly lady there is my grandmother. She's into rescuing everyone and everything. Gram loves company. It's probably more like she's keeping you captive."

"She's been telling us about growing up here on Honey Tree Farm. It's fascinating," said Maggie. "We hope we're not imposing. She's waiting for your grandfather, and we're waiting for Barry to pull our car out."

"Gram, you called Barry?" asked Travis. "He's about the slowest and most incompetent tow truck driver around. No wonder these poor folks are still waiting."

"We are enjoying her. Mrs. Sullivan has been telling us all about you and how you help take care of the bees."

"Gram, you're waiting for Grandpa?" said Travis. He took off his hat and walked over to her rocking chair. He put his hands on the arms of her rocker and looked her in the eyes. "You know we talked about this before."

"Travis, you go on home now. He'll be here soon. He's just out on a special errand."

"Have it your way, Gram," He shoved the cowboy hat back on his head. It was nice

119

meeting you folks. Sure hope you brought a
toothbrush. If you're waiting for Barry you
might be here all night."

Maggie laughed. "Could be. But Barry
called a while ago to say it wouldn't be long."

"One time a cow made him put his truck in
a ditch and he had to wait on someone to pull
him out." Katy giggled at this.

"Figures," said Travis. Maggie took Josh's
arm and tried to stop her own giggling.

"Folks, have a safe trip home, and if you
need me for anything my number is in the
little book by the phone."

"Gram, I love you, and stop kidnapping
people. I'll stop by in the morning and see if
you need to do any shopping." Travis stooped
to kiss the old woman on the forehead, patted
the dogs, and walked out the way he'd come.

"Travis, take the dogs out with you."
He gave a little whistle and patted his thigh.
The three dogs hurried to his side. Travis
waved once, shook his head with a smile and
headed out the door.

Maggie had calmed down. She picked up
her glass and took a sip of the tea.

"Oh my, let me put more ice in your glass."
Katy put her knitting down and started to get
up.

"Let me. You stay there and be
comfortable. Ice is in the freezer, I imagine,"
Josh said, walked around the table and
opened the refrigerator door. The light came

on immediately. He opened the short door at the top and found a bowl of ice. There were several rectangular pans with dividers and a handle. He pulled out the bowl and added ice to Maggie's and the other two glasses on the counter. He replaced the bowl and closed the doors.

"Mrs. Sullivan. Our refrigerator has an ice maker. I'll bet Travis or Jesse could install one for you. They are a real time saver."

"I'm used to the ice trays and I don't want to bother the men. Thank you for the suggestion. I'm not good at learning to use new fangled things."

"I love the things you've collected. You know how fond I am of antiques, and you have quite a few," Maggie said looking around. "What is that in the corner?"

"We called it a *mangle*. It's a Kenmore ironing machine. Jesse bought that for me thinking it would make ironing easier."

"It looks like a commercial unit with that large roller and the chrome cover." Maggie got up and went to it. "I imagine the roller revolves and the cover is the hot part that comes down over the piece you're ironing."

"It would steam too. That saved having to dampen all the clothes ahead of time. It was nice, but I don't use it anymore."

"You also have a coffee percolator and a clock radio. These must be from the 40s or 50s."

"Some are older, but that's pretty close. A few were wedding presents and others came from my parents or Jesse's."

Maggie walked back to her chair and sat down. "You have taken very good care of everything. I'm surprised they still work."

"Every now and then something will break or just stop working, but Jesse is very good at fixing things." Katy took a sip of her tea, and then sat the glass on the floor beside her chair. She rearranged the colorful bundle that would soon be Jesse's afghan and began knitting again.

"What happened next, Mrs. Sullivan?"

"Oh right, the prom... Well, it didn't quite go the way I'd hoped," she said. "But first came the wedding."

Chapter 18

When they weren't together Katy and
Jesse talked on the phone every night,
sometimes just listening to the other one
breath. The two families spent more time
together. Ted would help Jim work on the
rattletrap and the women laid out plans for
the wedding. Doris and Malinda scoured
cookbooks for party ideas. They studied Bride
Magazine, which Katy borrowed from the
library. The two women would turn the pages,
pick the dresses they liked best, and then
laugh heartily to think anyone would actually
pay those prices for a garment of clothing,
especially one that would only be worn once.

The third of April was Cora's birthday and
she had a small party at her house. She had
invited five girls from school and Katy. The
boys were from the football team plus Jesse.
Janice had come early to help set things up.

"Cora, put a tablecloth on the card table in
the den. We'll put the cake on it. Get the

napkins from the linen closet and the silverware," her mother said, trying to think if she had missed anything. "Janice, ice cream bowls are in the upper cabinet and..." She stood thinking. "I'll get the punch bowl and cups. If you'll get the punch - it's in the refrigerator in the big pitcher - and there's a plate of finger sandwiches there too. Oh, and the ice ring is in the freezer."

The three dashed off in different directions and at the stroke of two someone was knocking at the door.

"Hank, Jesse, you're right on time, and you're the first to arrive. Be careful, Mom might put you to work."

Just then she came around the corner wiping her hands on a kitchen towel.

"Hank, you're here just in time. Would you turn on the console and stack a couple 33 1/2s on? There is a Stan Getz and Guy Lombardo..."

"Mom! No," she turned to Hank. "Find the ones by Frank Sinatra, Bing Crosby and the Andrew Sisters."

"Yes, ma'am," he saluted and dragged Jesse with him into the living room.

Within a half hour everyone was there. Janice, of course, Karen Oliver and Carol Wheatley were in Cora's English class and Maize Goodrich was in her Algebra class. Hank and Jesse were joined by Carter Wentworth, Steve Fettig, Bill Brooster and

Bob DeWitt, all but Jesse played on the football team. Some brought gifts. Hank gave Cora a box of three hand crocheted hankies, while other gifts included perfume, bath power, a scarf, and a few Avon products. Everyone sang Happy Birthday and Cora had to blow out all eighteen candles if her wish were to come true.

As they sat around eating ice cream and cake there was a knock at the door. Cora's mother went to answer it.

"Are you here for the party?" she asked the young man.

"Yeah, I am," he said and brushed past her rudely. He went directly into the den where happy voices could be heard.

"Brice Bachlund! What are you doing here?"

The whole room became silent.

"I came to your party, of course." He strolled to the table and picked up a piece of birthday cake. "It wouldn't be a real party without me." He looked one by one at the other boys in the room as though he didn't want to forget who was there."

"I think you'd better leave," Hank said, and got to his feet.

A blanket of apprehension fell over the room.

"Are you telling me I'm not welcome here?" he said to Hank and took three steps toward him.

"That's pretty much what I'm saying. Yes," Hank stood his ground, looked him in the eye and didn't flinch.

"All my friends are here, but I'm not wanted? Is that what you're saying?"

"You heard me right."

Brice tried to jam the piece of cake in Hank's face but he ducked and it fell on the carpet. Brice almost lost his balance. Angrier yet, he turned on Hank again.

"You've been asking for it..."

"Stop it," Cora yelled. "Get out of my house!"

Brice heard but didn't take his eyes off Hank. Jesse jumped up and stood beside Hank.

"Touch him and you'll have to go through me, too." Jesse folded his arms across his chest and planted his feet, daring Brice to do anything.

"I mean it, Brice. Get out!" Cora was shouting. Just then her father came into the room.

"What's going on here?"

"Brice wasn't invited and he won't leave," Cora said.

"I think you'd better go, son."

Brice looked over the group again. "Who's going with me?" There was a long pause and Bill started to get up. Steve grabbed him by his belt and pulled him back down.

"I won't forget this!" Brice stormed out, not bothering to shut the door. He got in his car, gunned the motor causing the tires to squeal, sling gravel for yards and leaving gouges in the shale driveway.

"I pity the girl he's with tonight," Janice said. "Maybe we should warn her."

"He's not dating anyone from our school," Bob said.

"I don't know how we can stop him. He's such an ass," Jesse said.

"Someday he'll go too far," Katy said. "I feel kind of sorry for him."

"How can you feel sorry for a jerk like him, after what he's done?" Janice said.

"He's lost, like a little boy. I think he's angry inside and doesn't know how to deal with it," Katy said.

"I think he's a bully and enjoys hurting people," said Janice. "I'm sorry, I'll never forgive him!"

Katy hugged her friend.

Cora picked up the cake and tried to clean the frosting off the carpet with a napkin. Hank started the record player again and the kids began dancing. Soon they were having fun again and had all but forgotten Brice and the incident.

Jesse and Katy danced until the clock struck five. Holding Katy close, Jesse kissed her deep and passionately.

"Why, Jesse Sullivan, you can make a girl's toes curl," whispered Katy in his ear.

"Someday I hope to curl more than just your toes," Jesse whispered back.

Jesse and Katy left the party and headed home. He wanted to have her back to his house by five-thirty. As they pulled out onto the road, neither saw Brice parked among a clump of trees and watching them leave.

"Someday I'm going to get that goddam farm boy and his stuck up bitch, too." Brice growled out loud and hit the steering wheel with his fist.

"Oh Brice, why don't you just forget about them?" Nancy Crawford asked, as they left the movie that evening. Quick as lightning, Brice lashed out and hit her across the face, "Don't you ever tell me what to do!" Brice sneered and turned the key to start the engine. Nancy cowered in the corner, shocked at his sudden change.

"Brice you should take me home." He didn't respond but stomped on the gas peddle and squealed away from the curb. "Please!" Nancy asked.

"You'll go home when I'm ready to take you. Now shut up and let me think!"

Monday morning Janice and Cora were standing beside the lockers in the hallway when Alice Mountcastle walked toward them.

"Hey, did you hear about Nancy Crawford?
"Do I know her?" Cora asked.

"She's from Murdock High and had a couple dates with Brice."

"What about her," Janice asked.

"My neighbor goes to that school and is good friends with her. She said they were walking on the Jetty and Nancy slipped and fell over the rocks. She's badly cut up and she sprained her ankle."

"Did you say Brice was with her at the time?" asked Janice.

"Yeah," Alice said. "She told my neighbor it was an accident. She told her he kept her from getting hurt worse. I understand that her clothes were torn and she had blood all over her. What an awful thing to happen."

"I'll bet," Janice said. She pulled a book from her locker and slammed the door hard.

"Did he do anything else? Did he try anything?" Cora asked.

"When my neighbor asked, Nancy told her she doesn't want to talk about it. She told her 'just forget it. I have'. Wasn't that a queer thing to say?" Alice hurried away to her next class.

Cora grabbed Janice's arm. "What do you think?"

"You *know* what I think!"

"I wish we could do something. He's hurting girls and threatening them to keep quiet about it," Cora said.

"They're all afraid, just like me. I couldn't tell anyone but you. Come on or we'll be late for class."

As the girls hurried down the hall, they had to pass Brice and a group of his friends.

When they passed, Brice jumped out and yelled, "Boo." The girls jumped and scurried away. Brice and the others howled with laughter.

Saturday, May 8th arrived. Ted drove Doris to Jim's, picked him up and they left for the church. Flowers had been tied to the first six church pews. A white cloth ran from the alter to the double doors at the entrance in the back of the church. As friends and family came in Jesse and Ted ushered them along the white carpet to their pews. Jim stayed out of sight. He was so nervous he paced back and forth on either side of the baptismal font. When he tired of that he paced around it for a while.

The wedding was scheduled for five o'clock, and the women planned to arrive only five minutes early. This way Malinda would not have time to be nervous or have second thoughts. But the waiting was killing Jim.

Malinda's car came into view. Her brother, George, had driven the girls to the wedding. The car was festooned with streamers that fluttered in the breeze. George got out and opened the back door. Doris and Katy got out first. Katy wore a lavender sleeveless dress that complimented her blond hair. She carried a small bouquet of yellow roses and baby's breath, trimmed with a lavender bow. She stood to the side and waited for Malinda.

As the second hand moved closer to the twelve Ted looked in on Jim. He clapped his friend soundly on the shoulder, "There's still time to back out, old man," Ted said with a grin.

"You probably shouldn't say that right now," Jim said, and wiped perspiration from his brow.

"Take a deep breath and put one foot in front of the other. It will all be over in a few minutes. Before long you'll be living happily ever after. I think it says so in Grimm's Fairy Tales or somewhere."

Jim hesitated. "No one in those stories live happily ever after!"

"Whatever... You go first," said Ted. "I'll walk behind in case you faint."

Jesse joined them and the three men walked out of the baptistery and through the sacristy to the sanctuary. The red sanctuary lamp flickered joyfully overhead. Jim hesitated for a moment and Ted gently guided him to his rightful place in front of the communion rail. He looked out over the pews and saw that all six pews on either side of the aisle were filled with familiar faces. He sighed deeply and felt better.

The priest came out of the sacristy in his festive white vestments and book in hand. He nodded and somewhere in the back organ music began. A strong clear voice warbled a hymn of happiness and thanksgiving.

Suddenly Jim felt uncomfortable in his new clothes. His shoes felt too tight and the suit made him too warm.

At the end of the hymn the organ music changed to another hymn and Jim saw Katy come forward on the white carpet. A few steps behind Doris followed and then he saw Malinda. She held the arm of her brother George as they walked slowly up to join the men.

"It's okay to breathe," Ted whispered to Jim, who hadn't realized he was holding his breath.

Malinda looked like a model from the pages of Vogue magazine. Her ivory dress complimented her voluptuous curves. The hat and veil adorned her dark hair. The bouquet was a larger version of Katy's with yellow roses and lavender ribbons that cascaded down almost to the floor

Jesse was stunned when he saw Katy. He had never seen her look more beautiful.

The bride was handed over to Jim and wedding the ceremony began.

Jesse couldn't take his eyes off Katy and found himself imagining what it would be like if they got married.

The priest talked and talked but Jim didn't hear and certainly wouldn't remember anything but Malinda's smile. He recited when he was told to, exchanged rings on cue and heard the priest said, "I now pronounce you husband and wife. Jim waited to hear 'You may now kiss the bride', but he never did." The priest announced to the guests, "I'm pleased to introduce Mr. and Mrs. James Hailey." And then it was over and Malinda took Jim's hand and they led the procession out of the church.

Once outside the guests began clapping. The wedding party stood along the steps and shook hands with family and friends who congratulated and wished them well. A few even kissed them.

Everyone got into their cars and waited till the last of the well-wishers came through.

Katy gave Jesse a shy smile and walked to Sullivan's truck.

Jim and Malinda got into the car with George. He and the newly married couple led the parade of guests, who yelled and honked horns all the way to Malinda's house.

Jesse and Katy rode in the truck bed on a bail of hay loaded for that purpose.

"You look great," Jesse said, shouting over the clamor. Katy had to lean close to even hear him. They were happy just holding hands and sitting close.

All the trees around Malinda's bungalow had been decorated with streamers, and candles in glass bottles that hung from the branches. In addition to the recipes Doris and Malinda made, their friends and neighbors brought additional food. There were bowls of potato salad, platters of fried chicken, corn on the cob, homemade biscuits with apple butter and honey, rolls and sliced meats. There were platters of cold vegetables and bowls of hot vegetables, and like the miracle of the loaves and fishes, when some platter or bowl went empty another would appear miraculously from the kitchen.

A band had set up on the open back porch and tables of all sizes peppered the yard.

The weather was perfect and the sunset promised to be amazing. Magnolia and Jacaranda trees were bursting with color and Camellia blossoms filled the air with their heady fragrance.

Katy and Jesse walked along the path through the tables under the trees. They were decorated with fresh flowers matching the bride's bouquet. The center table held a three tier wedding cake. The kids took a seat at one of the tables and watched Jim and Malinda speaking to one and then another of the guests. The small band began to play softly.

After a while Malinda and Jim took their places at a table in the front. Jim was so happy and looked lovingly at his new bride.

He stood up and asked for quiet, "I want to thank everyone that helped us put this wonderful celebration together. Thank you for all the food you all brought, but no one can go home until every morsel is eaten."

The crowd laughed.

"The band is *Midnight Madness* and they know a lot of songs. I hope you will stay and dance. They promised to play a few slow ones for you old folks out there."

The guests roared again with laughter.

"Most of all I want to thank Malinda for becoming my wife today. We've spent a lot of years together - Katy and me - and Malinda is taking us both. I am so happy to be a whole family again."

Everyone stood clapping and cheering.

"I see most of you have found the nice assortment of honey brewed liquors and wines. For you Sissies, we also have some nice home brew. The crowd applauded heartily.

Ted stood up. "As best man, I'd like to make a toast to the newlyweds." He held up his glass. "We all know Jim as the county beekeeper. He finds the bees and builds the hives and shuttles them from farm to farm - great bees we will attest, but you'll have to agree that today he married a real *honey* and we wish them both the best!"

Everyone cheered, shouted, and drank from their glasses.

The thundering roar of a car engine caused heads to turn. The 1947 Ford coupe convertible screamed through the field beside Malinda's house, spraying grass and dirt on both guests and their cars. The horn blasted and music blared.

Brice spun his car in dangerous loops and laughing like a demented fool as the crowd run for cover.

"I'm calling the police," the priest said and disappeared into the house.

Jesse sprinted toward the car intending to stop this madness. Brice saw him coming and aimed the car straight for him. Jim got to Jesse and pulled him out of the way in the nick of time.

"He would have hit you!" Jim exclaimed. They all watched Brice's car make another loop then disappear down the road.

"He's going to push me too far one day!" Jesse turned and went back to the party.

Katy met him half way. "Are you nuts? Did you really think he would stop?" She grabbed Jesse and hugged him tightly; tears running down her cheeks. "Please, don't you ever do anything like that again. Do you hear me, Jesse Sullivan? Not ever!"

The police arrived with sirens wailing, but it was too late to catch Brice. They would pick him up later. Everyone knew his car. Sheriff Haywood and his men took statements from the guests.

"We can get him for disturbing the peace and reckless driving," Haywood said. "I'll have a talk with his dad again. Don't know how much good it will do. He's been protecting that kid for years and he has a lot of influence around here. Jesse, he's got it in for you. Don't do anything to provoke him, please."

"What about attempted murder?" Katy demanded. "He tried to kill Jesse. He was driving straight at him."

"I don't think Brice would go that far. I've got to file these reports, but I'll call in a couple of days to let you know how things stand. Brice will probably get off with a fine and probation. He always does. One day Mr. Bachlund won't be able to save him." Sheriff Haywood tipped his hat and walked back to his patrol car. He pulled out and headed for town.

"He almost ran my Jesse down. There is something seriously wrong with that boy," Doris said, sniffling.

The men in the wedding party went around to the guests encouraging everyone to stay and enjoy the food and the music. The band started up again and people gradually relaxed.

As nightfall came the candles were lit and everyone was mellow. The cake was cut, and Jesse and Katy helped hand it out to the guests.

Malinda stood on the porch near the band and threw her bridal bouquet over her shoulder to the waiting crowd of women that had collected in the yard. Jesse laughed at Katy's shocked expression as she looked down at the pretty bouquet in her hands.

"Looks like you're next," Doris said. "You know the old wives' tale, right? The one who catches the bride's bouquet is the next to go down the aisle."

The hour grew late. A few couples were still dancing, but most had devoured the food and drank their fill and little by little they had headed home.

"Malinda and I plan to take a couple of days at the beach on Anna Maria Island. We'll spend the night at my house. In the morning we'll return and remove all evidence of the celebration.

"You'll do no such thing. Tom, Jesse and I will take everything up for you."

George approached and caught the tail end of this conversation. "The family will help, too. There are enough of us, we'll have it removed in no time."

"Oh, thank you. Thank you all," said Malinda. She turned as Doris took her arm.

"One other thing," she said. May I make a suggestion? If you and Jim are leaving for a few days, why don't you let Katy stay at our house? She would be safer with us than alone in your house while that car salesman's son is running loose."

"That is very generous, Doris. I've never had to worry about her safety, but after today, I think you're right."

"Good. It's settled."

Some cleared the tables and pitched the garbage in a dry cistern on the back of the property. Everyone pitched in. Katy and Jesse stripped the tablecloths and put them in a pile for wash day. Two of the women removed the decorative lighting from the trees. The men moved the tables back in the house and those borrowed from neighbors were returned. In no time at all the work was done and everyone said their good-byes and went home. The only stragglers were Jesse and Katy, who it seemed never ran out of energy.

They were standing by Malinda's car when she locked the house and moved toward them.

"Katy, you're going to stay with the Sullivans while we're away. We'd rather you not be left alone right now." Jim said and helped Malinda into the passenger seat of her car.

"You want me to go with them right now?"

"Yes, we'll be leaving early in the morning and we will pick you up we get back," he said.

The kids almost burst with excitement. Katy quickly kissed Malinda and ran around to give Jim a peck on the cheek.

"You two, drive carefully, have a good time and I'll see you when you get back," she said, trying not to show how thrilled she was.

"I'll race you to the truck," Jesse said and took off running.

"Good-bye, I love you." She turned and ran after Jesse.

"Do you think she'll miss us?"

"Not a bit." They both chuckled. He turned the key in the ignition, pulled out of the drive and headed home.

Chapter 19

"You know I still have flowers from that bridal bouquet," Mrs. Sullivan said. She put aside the knitting, rose from her chair and stretched. "I loved them so much that I couldn't bear to throw them away. I pressed them in the old family bible along with a couple from my own bouquet." She went into the hall and quickly returned with the heavy bible. She sat it on the counter and slowly opened it. It was bulging from all the things stored inside.

There were a couple of dried yellow flowers with a faded lavender ribbon. Under it was a card about half the size of the book's pages.

"Is that the invitation Malinda made?"

"Oh yes, I've always cherished it."

"See?" she said, looking down at the dried buds. "I kept them all these years." Katy sighed, and for a minute she was far away in another place and time. Maggie reasoned she was remembering a world long ago.

As she turned the pages a photograph fell out. It was a picture of a young man and a pretty girl with blond hair.

"Is this a picture of you?" Maggie asked.

"Yes. Jesse and I were dressed for the prom. His father took it with a new camera that his father had purchased the year before. I think it was called a *Land Camera.* Maybe it was just supposed to take pictures of the landscape."

"Actually, I think someone named 'Land' invented it." Maggie said. "It must have been one of the early Polaroid models. Do you still have it? It would be worth a lot on today's market."

The old woman laughed. We have a lot of old things, but I don't imagine they have much value.

"Antiques are in high demand today. That's why shops like those in Arcadia are so popular."

Katy just chuckled. "Jesse's father took the picture of us just before we left to go to the dance."

"Is that where those flowers are from?" Josh asked, picking up a cluster of flattened roses.

Mrs. Sullivan let him hold it for a moment and then reached for it. She looked at it longingly for several minutes and then held it to her heart.

"I don't believe I ever had anything as beautiful as that corsage."

"It must have been from Jesse." Josh added, his voice soft.

"Yes, I got it that night."

"And you kept it all this time," he said.

"In the picture, the boy... Jesse is wearing a flower. Did you give it to him?" Maggie asked.

"No, I think Doris bought them both. He was wearing his when I arrived. Dad and Malinda drove me to their house. They said it was because they wanted to see Jesse too. Actually, Dad probably wanted to tell him when to have me home and such." She laughed. "My dad was like that."

"I see they took several pictures. Who is this?" Josh asked laying down a picture of three people.

"That one is Jesse with Ted and Doris." Katy tapped the faces in the picture with a gnarled finger that shook a little.

"Then this must be..." Maggie didn't finish the sentence as she laid another picture on top of it.

"Yes. That is me with Dad and Malinda." She picked it up for a closer look and a smile crept onto her lips. Then she laid it on the pile. "Ted had the camera loaded with a whole roll of film, and I thought at the time that he must want to use every bit of it." She chuckled, and added. "He was very proud. His

boy was grown up and taking a girl to a
prom."

The next picture was of her alone. Josh
noticed that she was standing at the stairway
by the phone. The pictures on the wall going
up the stairs looked very much the same as
they do now.

"How pretty you were!" Maggie added.

"That's the dress Malinda and I found. We
went shopping the weekend after her
wedding. We went to the same store on
Manatee Avenue and Mrs. Waverly helped us
find it."

"Were you nervous that there might be
another incident like the one with Brice the
time before?" Maggie asked.

"It did cross my mind," then she added
with a grin, "But I had Malinda with me. She
had grown up with boys and she knew how to
handle them."

The other two chuckled.

"It was pretty, but I struggled all evening.
The full skirt and high heels made it
awkward because I wasn't used to either.

"Here is one of Jesse alone. How cute he
was." Maggie laid the picture on the pile, but
Katy picked it up.

"Yes. He was attractive." She laid it down,
her hand shaking, but held onto it a moment
longer, as if unwilling to fully let go. "He was
so handsome in his rented tux. I remember
Ted clapped him on the shoulder and slipped

him a dollar bill, 'just in case you want to stop for ice cream'.

"What color was the dress?" Maggie asked.

"It was a midnight blue taffeta with a portrait collar that framed my face. Malinda had loaned me her pearl necklace and earrings. A trip to the beauty parlor was a treat. They piled my long hair up with cascading curls all around."

"It was very pretty," Josh added.

"Jesse went to the refrigerator and came back with the pink rose corsage. 'This is for you,' he said."

Mrs. Sullivan took a deep breath and sat up in her chair. "Oh my, I haven't fed the dogs yet," she said, looking around, "or have I?"

Maggie piped up, "I believe you already did, Mrs. Sullivan."

"I'm getting forgetful these days. My Travis worries about me. Isn't he a good looking young man? He looks just like his grandpa. You know, when I first met Jesse, I thought he was just about the neatest thing going. He was handsome, well built, and he went to a regular school. Don't get me wrong. I loved being home-schooled. My dad and I traveled around a lot after my mom died. He had to take the bees all over the county and home-schooling worked better for us. When Travis finishes high school, he's going to go to

college and learn the bee business. Jesse is so
proud of him."

Maggie and Josh looked at each other. The
Travis they met was mid-thirties at least.
Maybe she *was* getting forgetful.

"Mrs. Sullivan, what happened at the
prom?" asked Maggie.

"That was a night I will never forget. It
was a wonderful night and a horrible one. It
still plays over and over again in the middle
of the night."

Chapter 20

"Jesse drove Malinda's red Oldsmobile.

"We get to ride in style," Jesse said, while Katy was still adjusting her skirts. "We are meeting Cora, Hank and Janice there. All the guys will be jealous because I've have the prettiest girl with me."

"I feel like Cinderella going to the ball," Katy said, smiling.

"You look like Cinderella, and I am happy to be your prince."

"You *are* my prince, Jesse Sullivan," Katy scooted a little closer and took his hand.

They drove to the school and parked outside the gymnasium. The building was lit up and decorated all the way to the door.

Jesse looked at Katy, "You ready?"

"I'm a little nervous."

He reached over, took her hand and kissed it. "Come on, I want to show you off."

At the door Jesse handed his tickets to Miss O'Brian, one of the teachers.

"Hello, Jesse, who do you have with you tonight?" she asked.

"Miss O'Brian, this is my girlfriend, Katy Hailey."

"Hello, Katy. Welcome. I hope you enjoy yourself."

"Thank you, Miss O'Brian." Her voice cracked. She felt dry and cleared her throat. "It's nice to be here."

Walking along, Katy asked. "You introduced me as your girlfriend. Am I?"

"Of course you're my girlfriend, Katy," Jesse said, and taking her hand, raised it to his lips and kissed it.

"I'm glad," Katy gave Jesse a quick kiss on the cheek. He smiled and kissed her back.

The room was awash with crape paper, flowers and candles. Off to one side was a fancy arched bridge with columns at each end holding huge white globe lights. A couple stood on the bridge as a photographer took their picture. On another side was a colorful gondolier with a flat glass top that bore all kinds of food and bowls of punch. Several walls had big arches with life size statues painted in them. Big round tables with long white tablecloths topped with clusters of flowers and candles peppered the room. At the back was a stage filled with cardboard Cypress trees and a painted scene of the Italian countryside. Overhead were the words 'Venice, Italy'. Also on the stage a band of four musicians were playing. They were dressed in the black pants, horizontal black and white striped shirts, flat straw hats and a red sashes like gondoliers. Two ornate chairs and a lectern were set off to the side.

"Let's find the others," Jesse suggested.

She was taking in everything as she looked around. Were all schools like this? Even the doors were decorated. Several had black paper silhouettes of gondolas floating on canals of Venice. On the tables were travel brochures with scenes of Venice, Italy.

"Jesse, this is fabulous!" she gushed.

Cora and Hank waved from one of the tables to join them.

"This is Richard, my date," Janice said. Richard goes to Murdock High. They all greeted one another and took a seat.

"Isn't this fantastic?" Cora asked, looking around.

"I could never have imagined anything so beautiful. Who did all this?" Katy was still trying to take it all in.

"There was a committee of teachers and students who did it," Janice explained. "The whole senior class voted on a theme last September, and the committee has been working on it ever since."

"Wow, they must have all been studying art." Katy guessed.

"Well, no. But they did a great job." Janice smiled. "I was on the committee."

They all complimented her and gradually the conversation settled into small talk.

"Why don't we get the girls some punch?" Hank asked, and the boys left on the errand.

"Don't look now, but Brice is here. He's got a new girl with him." Cora put her open hand to her temple to either prevent him from seeing her or so she wouldn't have to look at him.

"Her name is Cassie Moore," Janice's tone turned sarcastic. "He must be getting desperate."

"None of the cheerleaders will go out with him." Cora said.

"Cassie is on the debate team and in math club." Janice just rolled her eyes.

"She's not one of the popular girls, Cora explained to Katy. "But she gets along with everyone."

"I think she's kind of cute," Katy noted.

"Even with those big cat's eye glasses!" Janice added sharply. "Still, we should warn her about him." Janice started to go, but Cora grabbed her arm.

"Wait! ...not until she's alone. We don't want to ruin the night for everyone with a big fight."

Brice was with a group of jocks, raucous and unruly. He noticed the three girls looking his way, and whispered something to his pals. Cassie looked shocked. She glanced over at Janice, then stormed off and sat alone at a different table. Brice followed her. They argued. Suddenly he grabbed her arm and dragged her back to his table.

"What's going on?" Jesse asked, as they handed punch to their dates.

"It's nothing important," Janice said, taking the drink from Richard.

The music changed to a faster beat, and everyone moved to the dance floor. At first Katy was stiff and self-conscious, but she soon relaxed and enjoyed the comfort of being in Jesse's arms.

The evening went quickly as the three couples talked, danced and snacked. The band played almost constantly until the announcement.

"We have come to that part of the evening in which we will choose this year's Prom King and Queen. Principal Miller, will you come up and do the honors?"

The whole room clapped as the principal waved to the crowd, climbed the steps and moved to the lectern.

"This is the good part," Cora whispered to Katy. "It's usually the most popular boy and girl in school."

"It's a very guarded secret," said Janice. Even those of us on the committee don't know who was chosen."

"Students, teachers and chaperones, as you know, the entire senior class chooses one girl and one boy in December. Those ballots are put in the safe and not seen again until

just before the prom. At that time, we count
the ballots. Miss O'Brian, Mr. Jarvis and I did
the counting behind closed - and locked! -
doors. The winner's names are in these sealed
envelopes."

He held them up - one pink and one blue
envelope - for everyone to see. A cacophony of
cheers, shouts, foot stomping and whistles
rocked the room. Mr. Miller was shouting into
the microphone just to be heard.

"I have the honor of introducing last year's
prom king, Clyde Henderson, who will read
the names of the winners." Clyde took the
stairs two at a time and swaggered
dramatically to the lectern as the cheering
continued.

The drummer gave a big drum roll, hoping
to be heard over the din.

Miss Toliver, the English teacher, held up
a cardboard crown, decorated with silver
paper, imitation jewels and a feminine cross
in the front. Mr. Manuel, the football coach,
held up the King's crown. It was decorated
like the Queen's crown except with a manlier
cross.

Mr. Miller held his hands up for silence. It
took several minutes, but the crowd finally
got quiet.

Miller made a great show of handing the
envelopes to Clyde. Then he stepped back and
all eyes were on Clyde. He held the girl's
envelope to his ear. When the crowd didn't

respond he shook it. There were a few titters from the audience before they realized he was teasing them.

"Open it!" someone shouted.

Clyde pointed to himself in a 'who me?' gesture.

"Yes! Open it!" the crowd shouted.

Clyde shrugged his shoulders and opened the envelope. He took the card out and read it silently and put it in his back pocket.

"Who is it!" the crowd shouted.

Clyde grinned and held it up. In the microphone he said, "Emily Hargrave is this year's Prom Queen!"

Cheers and shouts filled the room as Emily Hargrave walked to the stage. She shook hands with Clyde. Mr. Miller brought her a bouquet of roses and Miss Toliver handed the crown to Clyde.

"It is my honor to crown our new Prom Queen," and he set the crown on her head.

More cheers followed. There were tears in Emily's eyes, but she smiled and straightened the crown more securely. Clyde held the mic up to her.

"I just want to thank all the kids who honored me with this." She put her hand up in what might have been a wave or a signal that she was too emotional to say any more. She turned and took one of the thrones behind her.

Clyde held the blue envelope. He held it to his ear as before. There was no reaction. He shook it as if listening to what might be inside; still no reaction. He sighed visibly and opened it. Everyone was quiet. "This year's Prom King is - another drum roll - Clyde Henderson! Clyde clasped his hands and shook them over his head in a winning gesture. The crowd booed! Clyde dropped his hands, his expression - one of huge disappointment - as he schlepped to the lectern. Into the microphone, he said in a deep dramatic voice and each word growing louder...

"This year's Prom King is **Jesse Sullivan**!"

The crowd went crazy! Their reaction was deafening!

Those at his table cheered and laughed, clapping him on the back. Katy motioned him to leave, the crowd was waiting. He stumbled to his feet and hurried toward the stage. Kids congratulated him as he passed their tables. He got to the steps and hurried up. Clyde, the clown, had turned his back, was tapped his foot and checking his watch. Jesse had to tap him on the shoulder to let him know he'd arrived. Clyde grabbed Jesse's hand and raised it to signal his winning. The crowd reacted.

Mr. Manuel, brought the King's crown, and Clyde, with theatrical drama, placed it on Jesse's head.

There were shouts of congratulations, but it was too loud for anyone to hear anything. Clyde took Emily's hand and brought her to the forefront. He said something in the mic, but no one could hear it. The band played, but no one could hear that either. It's fair to say, the whole room was jubilant, well, almost the whole room. Clyde said something else into the mic, but his words were lost.

Emily and Jesse left the stage and rejoined their group. Jesse got to his table and took Katy's hand. He said something but she couldn't make it out. He walked her to the dance floor, were only Emily and her date and the two of them stood alone. The crowd gradually quieted and the music could now be heard.

"I asked for a prince and I got a king," said Katy, as he laid her head on his shoulder. They swayed to the romantic cords of *My Happiness.*

The room quieted completely. The crowd partnered and joined the couples on the dance floor, but Jesse and Katy could have been alone on a deserted island; they were only aware of each other.

Chapter 21

Brice had been watching the show. He was burning with anger and frustration. He should have been prom king. His buddies had all voted for him. They'd even thrown in a couple of extra votes. He hated Jesse, who had humiliated him, ruined things between him and Janice and called the cops on him at the wedding. Brice openly glared at the group.

"We're being watched," Cora said, nodding toward Brice.

"He has been all night," Janice added. "Richard, you don't know him, but he is more than mean; he's cruel and vicious. His dad's a big wig and the kid gets away with it every time. He beats up his girlfriends... he's just plain wicked."

When the music ended, they went back to their table. Jesse took off his crown and put it on Katy.

"I've never been a queen," she said. "Maybe I'll leave it on forever."

The group laughed and the boys went to get punch and snacks for everyone.

"Where's the restroom?" Katy asked.

"Come on, I'll show you," Janice said.

"No, that's okay. Point me in the right direction. I'll find it."

"Go to the doors where you came in and turn right. It's down the hall on the left past the water cooler. Sure you don't want company?" Cora asked.

"No, I'm fine. I'll be back in a minute. Here, you can guard my crown," Katy said, laying it down and waving to Jesse as he stood waiting in the line for punch.

Brice watched Katy leave and saw Jesse at the refreshment table. He meandered behind the tables and behind the kids on the dance floor. He saw Katy walk into the girl's restroom. He waited for her by the water fountain.

When Katy walked out she was brushing lint off her skirt.

"Well, well, if it ain't Jesse's little whore." Brice sneered, stepping in front of her.

Katy looked up, startled. Then fear set in. She was alone and knew what he was capable of. Even if she screamed, who would hear her with all the music and chatter in the gymnasium?

"Okay, I'm sorry," Brice said, changing tactics. "Maybe we can start over. How about I give you a little tour of the classrooms so you can see what a real school looks like?"

"Brice, I don't think that's a good idea." Her voice was shaky and it gave her away. She tried to step around him. "I have to get back. The others will wonder what's keeping me."

"Just one classroom..." Brice took her arm and pushed her across the hall to a door. "This is Miss Toliver's English class. She's teaching Romeo and Juliet now."

Katy felt it might be best if she went along with it. Maybe he would let his guard down, and she could get away quickly. She realized her mistake in the next instant. Brice led her into the classroom and locked the door behind him. Katy heard the click and her blood turned to ice.

"Now, Katy, don't be afraid," Brice said taking her by the shoulders and drawing her close. He whispered in her ear, "I only want what you've been giving out to Jesse."

"I don't do anything with Jesse; nothing like that!" She tried pushing him away.

"Of course you do," Brice said, lifting her skirt. Katy slapped his hands away, but he was much stronger. He pushed her to the floor and jerked her skirt up. She fought him, pushing and clawing. He rolled her onto her stomach and straddled her. With one hand he opened his buckle and unzipped his pants.

Katy screamed! "No, I've never done anything with Jesse! You can't do this!

"Stop fighting, you little bitch," Brice hit her so hard her ears rang.

She felt blood trickling down her cheek. Katy screamed. How could she stop him? She felt him shift his weight and her skirt was pushed over her head.

"Don't you know once a guy starts, he has to finish!" His hands were on her. He tore her panties. She screamed again!

The sound of breaking glass made Brice turn. Jesse reached through the broken glass and unlocked the door. The others were behind him.

Jesse launched at Brice knocking him over. Brice was on his back, his clothes in disarray exposing him. He rolled over and tried to get up.

The girls ran to help Katy.

Jesse knocked him back down with a punch to his eye. Brice winced, but came back swinging. Jesse pounded him fiercely.

Hank stood watching, shifting his weight from foot to foot, like a boxer eager to jump in.

Brice's lip was split and bleeding. The whites of his eye was already turning red.

Jesse grabbed him by his tie, swung a fist as hard as he could, connecting with his jaw and Brice fell back and laid still.

Jesse had his tie and was ready to swing when someone grabbed his arm.

"Enough, Jesse," Mr. Miller said, his calm voice sounding so out of place in this room so full of anger and violence. Jesse took a deep breath and let his arms fall.

Brice was coming around. Hank and Richard took him by the arms.

"Let him go, boys," said Mr. Miller. "You," he said, pointing a finger at Brice. "Straighten your clothes."

"Don't you know who I am?" Brice covers himself, tucking and zipping as he talks.

"You're a rapist who likes to beat up on defenseless girls." Hank said.

"Wait until my father hears about this. That little bitch wanted it. She asked for it."

"No I didn't. I begged you to stop," Katy said, her breath hitching.

"Boys," he said to Hank and Richard. "Take Brice to my office and stay with him. Do whatever you have to in order to keep him there. I'll call the police and Mr. Bachlund. The rest of you stay here, and I'll be right back."

Mr. Miller returned in a matter of minutes. "The police are on their way. We're still trying to reach Brice's father. Will someone please tell me what went on here?" They all started talking at once. "One at a time, please."

"Jesse since you were throwing the punches, let's hear your side. I gather that

160

Brice Bachlund was up to no good and you stopped him?"

"Yes, sir. He's had it in for me and my friend Katy for a while now. Mr. Miller, if we hadn't found her... You know what would have happened."

Jesse looked over at Janice, but she looked away. Nonetheless, Mr. Miller noticed the exchange.

They were interrupted by shouting and scuffling in the hall. Miller went to check. The police had arrived and were taking Brice to the station.

Brice was struggling. "I'm going to sue every one of you! Officer Jamison lost his grip on Brice took a swing him. The police pushed him to the floor and slapped handcuffs on him.

Brice was still shouting, "I'll get you for this. You won't have a job in the morning!"

They pulled him up and were walking him out. "You have the right to remain silent, you have the right to an attorney..."

"You!" Brice shouted at Jesse as he was pushed along. "Don't think I'll forget this."

"Oh, will he come after us, Jesse?" Katy was worried.

"Nah, he won't get out of it this time. The police have him now."

Cora pulled Janice into the hall. "We need to talk."

Jesse put his arms around Katy. He drew her close and kissed her on the forehead. "Are you okay? I'm so sorry. I never thought Brice would try anything tonight with everyone around. Your father is going to kill me." Jesse handed her the handkerchief from his pocket to wipe the blood from her lip. She wiped it gingerly.

"The girls offered to come with me, but I said no. I didn't even think about Brice."

"How does your face feel? You've been cut. We'll have to talk to the police. Should we call your dad?"

"No. Let's tell Dad when we get home. Brice has ruined enough of this night."

"Whatever you say," Jesse continued.

"How did you ever find me? I knew he wasn't going to stop. I didn't know what else to say to him. I just kept screaming."

"The girls noticed that Brice was gone. The guys helped me look for him. I heard you scream." He kissed her. "You've got good lungs, girl... Thank God."

Mr. Miller returned. "The police have taken Brice to the station. Do you feel like talking to them tonight?"

"Do I have to?" Katy wiped her eyes.

Jesse looked at Katy. Her dress was torn, her hair was a mess and her cheek was cut and bruised. "Could we go to the station in the morning?"

"Yes, I'll suggest that to Sheriff Hayward. He's very understanding. But be prepared for a lot of questions." Mr. Miller started to leave. "Brice was talking about pressing assault charges against you, Jesse. Hank and Richard told us what they had seen though. That will get you off the hook. They also filled us in on how Brice has been harassing the two of you, and there will be enough witnesses from the wedding, I understand." He looked at the faces of the kids. "The officer took statements from Hank, Richard, Cora and Janice. It looks like Brice will serve jail time for this one. Mr. Bachlund was not happy when I spoke to him just now. He'll see Brice at the police station."

They thanked Mr. Miller and he left.

"I wish we could go back to the dance."

"I wish we could too," Jesse said, and took her hand. "I wish we could dance all night and into daybreak and forget this whole awful incident."

She kissed him.

"We'll have to bring our parents tomorrow. We can't shield them from what's been happening any longer."

Katy slipped into the restroom to tidy up while Jesse and the boys waited in the hall.

"Thanks for standing up for me." Jesse rested against the wall, rubbing his sore and bruised hands. He had a cut over one eye and would have a black and blue shiner for weeks.

163

"Brice deserves all the jail time he gets," Richard replied.

Katy joined the boys. Quick footsteps and chattering caused them to turn. The girls were running toward them.

"Everyone heard Brice shouting and that he's been arrested." Cora said, a little breathless.

"Cora said that I should be tough now and tell the police what Brice did. And then several girls came up to me. They kind of knew what had happened to me, because something like that had happened to them too. They offered to give statements. If we all talk to the police now, they'll listen. We want Brice stopped! Together we can make it happen."

Jesse opened the door of Malinda's car for Katy. But instead of getting in she turned to him.

"Kiss me, my king."

He pulled her close. His lips pressed hers, his tongue encouraging her to open her mouth to him. He sighed when she surrendered to his touch. He felt a heat build and his pants were becoming too tight. He wanted more, but...

Parting, Katy whispered, "You make my toes curl."

"I can't even tell you what you do to me," Jesse said, holding her.

HONEY TREE FARM

Chapter 22

The dogs announced the arrival of Katy and Jesse when they drove up into the yard of the Sullivan farm.

"Hi," Ted called out, hearing the screen door open. Jesse took Katy's hand. There was a moment of hesitation, a moment to prepare for the conversation that was bound to follow. Jesse squeezed Katy's hand and they proceeded into the kitchen.

"Did you have a good..." Ted stopped in his tracks when he saw them. "Oh, my god! What the hell happened?" Ted didn't wait for an answer. He called up the stairs. "Doris, wake the Haileys, they need to come downstairs."

He pulled out a chair and gestured for Katy to sit. He reached up to touch her bruised and swollen cheek, but didn't. "My dear child. Your folks went to bed a while ago. Doris will bring them down. Can I get you anything?"

"I... I'm fine, now." She squeezed Jesse's hand to bolster her courage. She was on the verge of tears, but didn't want to cry. That would just make things worse.

Doris reached the bottom of the stairs with Jim and Malinda right behind her. The three rushed to the kitchen.

"What is the urgency?" Doris asked, then she saw them. "My God!"

All three stopped abruptly in the doorway when they saw the kids, who only hours ago had been clear-eyed and happy. Now they were bruised and bleeding and their clothes were torn and disheveled.

Doris was the first to speak, but all that came out was... "What...?"

Jim went to his daughter. "Did you have an accident? Are you all right? What happened?" The last words broke up and his voice cracked.

"Thank God, you're all righ..." Malinda began but broke down before she could finish.

Jesse spoke softly. "Maybe you should all sit down."

The families sat around the kitchen table and Jesse and Katy told them all that had transpired. Their account took the listeners from the thrill of the event, the beauty of the room, how they danced and won the Prom King crown, and then the storm clouds rolled in when Katy disappeared, the search for her, breaking into the locked room, and the fight that ensued, the police, the Brice screaming, hitting the officer and finally being hauled off in handcuffs to jail.

The room was dead silent for a very long moment as each tried to grasp the full significance of what had happened.

Malinda, who sat next to Katy took her hand, but she was too disquieted to speak.

Jim felt no such calm. He burst out of his chair and went to his daughter. He brought her to her feet and wrapped his arms around her. "I could kill that son of a bitch, I could kill him!" He held her, tears spilled down his cheeks. The words hitched in his throat as he rocked her gently. "I could just kill him."

Malinda went to them and put her arms around both of them. "No, killing would be too good for him. We will see him in jail and away from descent people."

In the meantime, Tom sat with his down and his hand over his eyes trying to deal with all he had heard, or maybe he didn't want them to see his eyes.

Doris went to Jesse. "How are you?" she asked, gently touching his eye checking the damage.

He smiled, but his eyes were more truthful. "Better, now that we're home. The bruises and cuts will heal, but the memory of seeing him on her when we broke in; I don't think I'll ever be able to forget that."

She hugged him and kissed his cheek. "I'm very proud of you."

Tom now stood at his side, his own face wet with tears and his eyes red. "We are both proud. No matter what happens now we will be beside you - both of you - all the way."

"Brice is the one in for a bad time. We will talk to the police tomorrow and file formal charges. Sheriff Haywood felt we should come home tonight and speak to him in the morning.

"He's a good man. He understands that you'd want your parents with you when you talk to him."

"Janice, Cora, Hank and Richard gave statements, each telling what they saw," Katy said.

Jim kissed Katy on the forehead. "How are you feeling?" He looked her over inspecting her cheek and bruises. "Doris, why don't we put a little honey on their cuts? It will help them heal."

She nodded and went to the cupboard. Inside she brought out a lidded jar. As the family talked she smeared each of their wounds with a dab of the golden fluid.

Jim rose to his feet. "It's getting late and tomorrow will be another stressful day. I suggest we all get some rest."

The others agreed.

"First I am going to take a hot bath. My skin crawls at the thought of that lunatic touching me."

"I'm going with Katy when she presses charges," Jesse said.

"We all will," Malinda said and squeezed his hand. "Then we shall say good night, too." She kissed Katy on the cheek, turned and took Jim's hand. The two of them headed for the stairs.

Jim turned again. "You're sure you're all right, Katy girl?"

"Dad, in spite of all that's happened," Katy said, taking Jesse's hand and looking him in the eye, "The good part was the best night of my life."

Jim smiled, "I guess that's what I needed to know."

"It's been a long night," Doris said, "We all need to rest and we'll tackle whatever comes in the morning.

Jesse, Katy and both sets of parents went into the police station on Main Street. The clock on the wall read 9:40 when they were shown into a room to wait for the Sheriff.

Malinda took Katy's hand. "Are you nervous, dear?"

"Not about pressing charges. He needs to be stopped, but I just hope I don't have to see him or talk to him."

"If that should happen, we're here for you. He will never get the chance to hurt you again," Jim said.

Katy could see the pulse in her father's cheek; he was gritting his teeth, a familiar sign that he was holding his temper.

The door opened and Haywood walked in with a woman.

"Katy, this is Mrs. Jackson. She will take your statement. Do you want to speak to her privately?"

"No, sir. My family is with me and I'd like them to stay."

"Very good. I'll leave you then. But in the meantime I want to talk to Jesse. He turned to Jesse. "Come with me please. You may bring your parents if you like."

He held the door as the three walked out into the hall.

"Let's go in here where we can talk. Haywood opened the door to a similar room; they entered and took seats around a table. Haywood sat across from Jesse.

"I want you to tell me everything that happened last night from the time Katy left the group and be specific."

For the next hour and a half they repeated in detail the incident as they remembered it. The emotion in the rooms oscillated around anger and tears to strength and determination. At the end, papers were signed and Jesse and Katy, quite exhausted, were allowed to leave.

"What will happen to Brice now?" Katy asked.

171

"We will hold him over the weekend. The arraignment will take place on Monday, at which time bail will be set. That will determine if he is released or held."

"I hope he never gets out. He scares me!" Katy took Malinda and Jim's hands. She needed their strength. She wished she were 5 years old again, a time of innocence and before any kind of fear crept into her life.

The Haileys met the Sullivans in the hall. Jesse went to Katy. He put his arms around her and held her for a long moment. The worst was over, for now. At first a single tear trickled down her cheek, but she could be brave no longer; she burst into tears and the sobs that followed jarred the others as well.

It was a long heartfelt moment before anyone spoke.

"Why don't we take the children to the cafe down the street? They've been through a lot and need a change of atmosphere... and something to eat," Doris took Tom's hand, but spoke to Jim and Malinda. With Jesse's arm around Katy, they all left the station and walked out into the bright Florida sunshine.

The weekend passed with only a few moments of anxiety and a couple of bad dreams. Sheriff Haywood said he'd call the families with news of the arraignment as soon as he knew anything.

The phone in the Hailey's house rang just after 3pm. Jim answered it.

"It didn't take long and Brice has been formally charged. The judge set the bail at $25,000. That's quite high, but Mr. Bachlund was able to come up with the money. Brice has been released into his father's care."

"No! How could he do that?"

"The judge told Mr. Bachlund to keep his kid at home. Any further incidents and the bail will be revoked and forfeited."

"I don't know..." Jim said. "I'm going to keep my gun handy. If that kid comes after my daughter again, I can't be held responsible for what happens."

"Go easy, Jim. You *will* be held responsible if anything happens. I know the kid's trouble and I intend to keep a close eye on him too. Maybe you could stay with friends for a while. Most likely he will be homebound, but if you're concerned you might leave for a while."

Twenty minutes later the phone rang again and Jim answered it.

"We just got a call from Haywood. He said he talked to you."

"Katy is beside herself with fear, Tom. Malinda and I are worried too. I don't know how they could free him; they know he's dangerous!"

"I know. We feel the same. Doris and I think you should all come over here and stay with us for a while."

"I don't see how that can help. I should be here, just in case."

"We'd really like to have you. I think we'd all feel safer. You know safety in numbers and all that."

"I'll think about it." Jim hung up. He heard Katy and Malinda talking in the kitchen. He could tell from their tone how afraid they both were. "What am I going to do?" he asked himself. He took a deep breath and headed for the kitchen.

Chapter 23

The Haileys arrived at the farm that evening.

"This is just for a night or two," Jim said to Tom as they came up the porch steps. "Just to give my women some peace of mind; then we go back home. I don't want to be a burden."

"You'll stay as long as you need to," Doris replied. Jesse ran past her to help carry their things in.

The evening was more comfortable than any of the past several days. The adults played dominoes and drank coffee. Jesse and Katy played with the dogs on the porch.

"Watch Barker," Katy said and tossed the ball to Midge." They both laughed when the competitive Springer Spaniel overtook the slower mutt, Midge, who snatched the ball. Toby, jumped up trying to take the ball away, but the larger dog was too smart for him.

"It's getting late, kids." Malinda said, as she came to the screen door. "We have church tomorrow so we'd better get some sleep."

175

The house was quiet except for the typical nightly sounds. The clock on the dresser ticked away the seconds. The limb of the Crape Myrtle scratched the living room window in the rising wind. The refrigerator produced a constant hum and somewhere in the distance was the hoot of an owl.

Barker sat up, his ears alert and listening. Then the other dogs heard it and they started barking. They ran, circling and scratching at the door. When they got it open they raced down the stairs barking an alarm.

Jim and Ted were the first ones down the stairs.

"Easy," Ted called at the dogs, who were scratching at the kitchen door.

"What is it?" Jim asked.

"I don't know," Ted opened the door and the screen door and stepped out on the porch. The dogs flew out the door, down the steps and headed for the orange grove.

As Ted and Jim followed the dogs into the yard, they saw taillights fishtailing onto the road. Then they smelled it. Smoke! Billowing smoke was rising over the trees, but the flames were sporadic, a little here, a little there. The barn was alive with the sounds of bellowing cows and barking dogs.

Tom ran back into the house, "Fire! The grove is on fire," he yelled. "Doris, call for help! Jesse, you and Katy come help.

"The bees!" Katy said racing down the steps. "What about the bees?"

"Jesse, get to the fence and start the hose," Tom yelled. Do what you can to wet the trees. Katy and Malinda, check the barn. If there's fire there get the cattle and chickens out. Otherwise grab some buckets, use the water in the trough to fight the fire till help arrives."

They all ran to their assignments. Tom caught up with Jim.

Jim was panting. "Several hives are totally engulfed. We're going to lose them all. The smoke will taint the honey and we can't get close enough to save them. What's worse, the heat and flame will set the barn on fire."

"We'll hose down the barn and maybe that will minimize the damage there. Then we need to work on the trees. They're green and won't catch fire easily, but that's only a guess. It will depend on what accelerant was used and how quickly we get help. We have to keep the fire from taking hold and destroying everything!"

Adrenalin was high and they all worked as quickly as possible. Jim took the hose and tried spraying the hives, but the fire was hot and the flames too high. He turned the water on the barn. Some of the boards were already aflame, but as long as the water ran down the wall the flames failed to take hold.

Doris and Malinda had water buckets and were trying to wet down the edge of the fire to keep it from spreading. The fire was too hot to get any closer.

Ted was on the fence spraying the trees. Jesse was on another hose spraying trees he could reach. The smell of gasoline was strongest near the hives. That was probably were the fire started. A line of burnt ground left no doubt that the gas had been taken from the hives to the trees. They worked steadily, wiping perspiration and smoke from their eyes in the warm May night. Finally, they heard sirens approaching.

The pumper and a rescue truck raced through the yard, past the house and to the barn side of the grove. Tom jumped down and met Jeff Gardner, the rural fire chief. He quickly pointed out what they had accomplished. The four firefighters were well rehearsed and got their equipment up and working in a matter of minutes. Jeff shouted instructions to his team and to the civilians. They acted quickly and got the fires out before everything was ruined.

Jesse took charge of the hoses and put them back in their places. Katy and the women rounded up the buckets and put them away, refilled the trough, checked and calmed the cattle in the barn. As the emergency abated and the work of putting things back came to an end, exhaustion took over.

"Jeff, come have a glass of something cool before you head back. Please," Doris wiped her forehead with the back of her hand.

"We'd like that, Mrs. Sullivan."

Tom and Jim stood off to the side inspecting the damage to the hives.

"Jim, I'm so sorry."

"Tom, this might never have happened if we hadn't been staying here."

"Nonsense, it would have happened here or at your place. We both know who did this. He might have set fire to your house if you'd been home and asleep in your beds! The things that saved us here were the dogs and all of us working together."

"We've lost the hives," Jim was saying to Tom when Katy approached. "We'll have to start you over with some new ones."

"Thanks. Next time we won't set them so close to the barn." Tom and Jim both chuckled at that, more from irony than glee. Katy just shook her head.

"Men."

"Let's go inside. I'll call the police," Ted said. Jesse caught up with them as they walked back to the house.

"Jesse," Katy said as he stepped into the kitchen. He stopped and turned to her. "Look at you all sweaty and smudged with smoke."

He chuckled, "Me? Have you looked in a mirror lately?" He pulled her close. "But you look good to me even if you are all sweaty and smudged with smoke... and stinky." She laughed.

"My King, newly back from fighting with the fire breathing dragon."

Tom was on the phone as it rang into the station. The clock read 8:46. "Hello, this is Tom Sullivan. Is Sheriff Haywood coming in today?" There was a short pause as he listened to the night Sergeant. "Well, get hold of him and tell him that someone tried to burn down my barn and orchard. Have him come by and see for himself. Yes, we'll be here."

Jeff walked into the hall just as Tom was hanging up the receiver on the round base rotary dial phone. "I will have to make a report and our arson investigator will come by and look at the damage too."

"Thank you, Jeff. We owe you a debt of gratitude." Tom said, shaking his hand.

"Well, your wife has fed my men so many cookies they won't be worth a wooden nickel till they get a nap." Both men chuckled.

Jesse, Doris, Malinda and Jim sat at the table drinking coffee and eating cereal.

"Come have a cup. You look like you need it," Doris said patting the place next to her at the table. "Katy is taking her bath now. We'll all follow in turns and then naps are in order all around. Jesse you go next."

"Okay, if I happen to fall asleep at the table, just push me over on the floor. I'll probably sleep till September." He yawned hard enough to make his jaw crack.

Just then Katy called from the head of the stairway, "I'm finished. The bathroom is clear."

"That's my signal," Jesse said and kissed his mom. "I'll see you all later."

Jim waited until he heard the bathroom door shut. "We saw someone driving off across the yard and out to the road. That someone is the culprit. We couldn't see the car, but we saw the taillights."

"There's no doubt in my mind," said Tom. "It was the same car that harassed us at the wedding."

"You think it was Brice Bachlund?" Doris asked, her eyes wide with surprise.

"I do."

"But Tom, he's ordered to stay at home or his father is out of all that money."

"You expect a boy like that to obey his father?"

"But, wouldn't his father..." Jim interrupted her.

"That boy has no respect for anyone, and his father has never been able to control him. He probably just waited for his father to go to bed, slipped out of the house..."

"He could easily have gotten his hands on the gasoline to set the fire." Tom added.

"All he had to do was drive into the yard and to the barn. Who would have seen him at that hour?"

"Thank God for the dogs." Tom took another sip of his coffee. "I can only imagine what would have happened if they hadn't awakened us."

Almost as if those words were a command the dogs began barking again. Tom looked out and saw Hayward's cruiser had turned into the driveway and stopped in front of the porch. Haywood opened his door and stepped out. His passenger, a young officer got out too. The dogs raced from one to the other giving each their equal attention.

Tom walked down the steps and shook Haywood's hand,

"Hi, Burt. Sorry to have to call you out on a Sunday morning. Obviously you got my message."

"That's what they pay me for, little as it seems sometimes," Haywood said with a grin. "What happened here?"

Tom and Jim took him out to the orchard. They showed him the damage to the trees, hives and barn. They told him they were sure whose car it was that drove off. Sheriff Haywood jotted notes in a notebook while the younger officer took pictures. Freddie here will get statements from the women, but I'd like the two of you to came down and make a full report." He signaled the officer to go.

"Brice just keeps digging himself in deeper. The attempted rape charge is bad enough, but breaking bail, and now arson. If he's not careful he might never again see daylight outside of a prison."

"I'm not so sure. His father will get him a good lawyer." Jim said. "Time will tell, I suppose."

The rest of the day was spent catching up on lost sleep. Even the dogs remained quiet. Jesse thought he was the first one up until he found Katy sitting on the fence near the burned hives. The smell of smoke and burnt wood from the trees and hives hung heavily in the air. Katy's cheeks were moist from crying. "The poor bees." Her hair hung down, washed but not brushed out. "Dad will replace the hives. I don't know what they'll do with the trees."

"None were ruined. I imagine several will have to be trimmed but they'll grow back for next season."

"This is my fault."

Jesse pulled Katy off the fence and shook her by the shoulders. "Don't you dare think that, Katy Hailey! This is *not* your fault! We know Brice did this; it's his fault! He's a spoiled brat and a bully, who likes to hurt people. His father has let him get by for so long, his kid thinks he's untouchable.

"Jesse, don't be mad at me."

He pulled her close and wrapped his arms around her.

"I'm not mad at you, my dear one. I love you, and the thought of that... that son of a ... well, I can't bear him hurting you. But it does make me angry that you would blame yourself. He loosened his hold on her and kissed her gently to reassure her. "Katy, I love you and always will. We will replace the trees and the hives, and the barn, if we have to. But there would be no replacing you. What Brice tried to do to you is unforgivable. He's mad at me and taking it out on my family and me. He's picks on you because he knows it hurts me." Jesse kissed her again. Katy laid her head on his shoulder and clung to him with all her strength.

"Can I ask you something?"

"You can ask me anything, Katy Hailey."

"Can we go to another dance one day? I liked dancing with you."

Jesse hugged her tightly, "Of course we can."

"Thank you, my King."

Chapter 24

The next few months passed in a blink. The Haileys returned to their own home, which both Jesse and Katy hated to see. Brice was sent away pending his trial; set for September. Caps and gowns and graduation took place the second week in June, followed by graduation parties at the homes several of the seniors.

Jesse reminded Katy each time that these parties were not the party he had promised her. She would have to be patient because the time had to be perfect for her perfect party.

All apprehension was gone with Brice out of the way. The trips to the police station, giving depositions, filing charges, speaking to attorneys filled much of their free hours, but it also contributed to their comfort hearing what would likely happen to the culprit.

On a Sunday in July, the Sullivans were sitting around the kitchen table.

"There's still coffee in the pot; anyone for more? There are a few donuts leftover. Help yourselves," Tom said.

"None for me, thank you." Doris got up and stretched. "I need to get up and move before I take root here in this chair. I want to check the garden anyway." She kissed Tom on the cheek and grabbing her cloth gloves from the nail headed out the back. The dogs eagerly joined her.

"Jesse, we need to have a talk." He cleared his throat. Tom crossed and uncrossed his legs twice before he seemed to get comfortable.

Jesse could see that his dad was nervous and unsure how to begin whatever it was he wanted to say.

"Jesse," he began again. "You and Katy have been spending a lot of time together. I've seen how you are with each other." He cleared his throat again.

"Yes," Jesse said.

"Is there anything we should know about?"

"Like what, Dad?"

"Well, you've been spending a lot of time going to parties, and other things."

"I'm not sure what you're getting at, Dad."

Tom cleared his throat a third time. "Let me begin again." He opened his mouth, but then shut it and shifted once more in his chair.

"Dad, if you're wondering if we've had sex, the answer is no." Jesse felt his face turn hot and knew it must be a crimson red.

"Oh, good." Tom was instantly relieved - not that they hadn't had sex - but that this conversation would soon come to an end.

"Katy is a good girl. She has been sheltered and it wouldn't do for you to talk her into anything she's not ready for."

"Dad," Jesse explained. "Katy and I have known each other for years and somewhere along the way we fell in love. We know we'll get married one day and then we'll have babies by the dozens, but not yet. Dad, she's a lot smarter than anyone knows. She can see into the heart of a person and find the good buried there; even Brice. She sees beyond the bully and the spoiled brat. She sees a lonely and frightened kid desperate to gain his father's love. But he's a father, who can't show love, and thinks giving things will make up for it." Jesse put his coffee cup down. "We talk a lot and I can see what she sees. I love her, Dad. I would never hurt her or do anything she is not ready for."

"I don't know what to say, Jess." Tom rubbed the stubble on his chin. "You have grown up so much. Just when did that happen? You are wise for your years and you have things pretty well covered. Just do me one favor. Think about consequences before you and Katy jump into anything. Your mother is worried that... God, this is hard. She's worried you might get Katy pregnant. There I said it."

"Dad, I'm not going to rush into anything. I respect Katy too much. Now can we change the subject, please?"

Jesse put his cup in the sink and went to his room.

Doris opened the screen door and came in removing her gloves. She and the dogs stood for a moment. Then she went to the sink and washed her hands. She wiped them on a towel. "Did you talk to him? What did he say?"

"Don't ever ask me to do that again. From now on you do your own questioning." Ted filled his cup with coffee that had now gone cold. "Yuck," he said, sipping the disgusting brew. He poured the coffee in the sink. "I don't think we need to worry about Jesse and Katy."

"What do you mean?" Doris whispered.

"He's not a child any more. He thinks more clearly than anyone I know. More than some adults I know."

Chapter 25

The sound of an approaching motor interrupted the story.

"Well, land sakes, it's about time!" Mrs. Sullivan struggled out of the rocker and walked to the kitchen door. The dogs raced out barking wildly at the newcomer.

Josh and Maggie followed them to the driveway.

"You the people with the car in the ditch?"

Barry was a big black man with a lopsided grin and salt and pepper hair and wearing a worn baseball cap. He extended his hand to greet the couple, then realized how greasy they were. "Sorry folks. It's been one of those days." He wiped his hands on his coveralls.

"I got your car on the flatbed back there. I know a garage on the Tamiami Trail just outside Bradenton that will hold it over the weekend. That'll give you time to contact the rental agency. Maybe you have someone you can phone to pick you up? It's getting late, but the guy lives next to his garage. That makes it handy in situations like this."

"My parents are waiting to hear from me. I didn't know what to tell them, you know, if the car was drivable or not."

"Maybe they might meet us at the garage?" He took off the cap and scrubbed his hair with his fingers. "I can wait there with you for a spell, but it's been a truly tiresome day."

"I understand and I'll call them right away. That's terrific, thank you."

Katy saw Maggie's expression change.

"What is it child?" the old woman asked gently.

"I'm just disappointed. I wanted to hear the rest of the story."

"I tell you what, young lady," Barry spoke up. "I haven't had a bite since breakfast. If Miz Sullivan's got anything to eat, I'll be happy to wait and let you finish that story you're so anxious to hear."

Katy's eyes lit up.

"You know, Barry, I've got some ham and I'll make you a couple sandwiches. You sit right down. All of you, sit.
I've got potato salad, homemade pickles and my special honey tea. I think we still have some of Jesse's apple pie."

She rummaged through the refrigerator and pulled out a number of things. "That's just what we'll do. Would that do you for a spell Barry?"

190

"Oh yes, Miz Sullivan, you are a kind and generous woman, and I believe you're the best cook in Desoto, Hardee and Manatee Counties," he chuckled. "How could I possibly say no to an offer like that? Mind if I wash up first?"

"Sure thing, it's in the same place it's always been."

Barry went to the half bath just off the kitchen as Mrs. Sullivan made his sandwiches.

"Can I help you?" Maggie asked.

"You can get down a plate and glass from over there, and pour him some tea."

Barry came back and took a seat at the table.

"The front axle is broken on your car. I got it out of the ditch and up on the truck. It nearly tipped over on its side once."

Maggie handed Barry his tea.

"Thank you, mam." He nearly emptied the glass then gave a big sigh. "You have no idea how good that is to me."

"Can the car be fixed?" Josh asked.

"Oh, Mose can fix anything. Yes, sir. But no telling if he has the parts and such. But that will be up to the rental company to deal with."

"Okay," Josh got up. "I'll call Dad and have him meet us. Barry, would you mind coming with me? They are going to need directions."

The two men disappeared down the hall to make the call and returned just as Katy was putting the plate on the table.

"Here's what the doctor ordered." She grinned.

"Thank you, very much." He took one of the sandwiches in both hands took a quarter of it in a single bite.

"I'll just cut us all some of that apple pie I baked for Jesse this morning. It will surely be gone if he doesn't get home soon," she said with a chuckle.

Barry tilted his head and stopped chewing. He looked around at the group at the table.

"Miz Sullivan? You okay?" he asked.

"Right as rain, Barry, thanks for asking. Just telling these folks the story about how I came to be at Honey Tree Farm."

"Ma'am, has Travis been by lately to see you?" Barry asked. He put the sandwich down.

"Why, yes. He was here earlier. He said he'd take me shopping in the morning." She made sure everyone had a glass and filled each one with ice and tea, than sat down in her rocker and closed her eyes for a moment.

Chapter 26

It was several weeks before Jesse and Katy heard from Sheriff Haywood again. It was near the end of July when he phoned the Hailey house to give them good news.

"The District Attorney is ready to proceed with the trial in September," he stated. "Brice's father sent him to live with an aunt in Brooksville. Guess he's hoping to keep him out of trouble until the trial. Two more girls have come forward with statements that he beat them and either tried or *did* molest them."

"That's wonderful news," Jim said, smiling at Katy and Malinda, who were eagerly standing nearby.

"Katie's friend, Janice came into the station with her mother a couple of days ago and added her statement. That one is of great importance. She's willing to swear in court that he beat and raped her. That will certainly help our case. All the girls who came forward have agreed to testify."

"Do you know where the trial will be held?" Jim asked.

"Mr. Bachlund hired an attorney from Jacksonville. He requested a change of venue to Tampa. He feels getting a fair and impartial jury may not be possible here. The Judge is Walter H. Dexter. He's good and has handled a lot of criminal cases. Matthew Coffee is the Assistant District Attorney assigned to prosecute."

"Is the trial still set for September?" Jim asked.

"Yes, but the defense attorney is dragging his feet. He knows he's going to find it hard to get around all the evidence."

"Thanks for letting us know," Jim said, and hung up the phone.

"Let's go talk to the Sullivans," Jim said. "They'll want to know what's been said."

Doris was watching Jesse as she puttered around the kitchen.

"You're awfully quiet. What's on your mind?" She asked him as she wiped the counter top with the wet towel she'd been drying dishes with.

"Mom, am I doing the right thing, going off to college? It's a lot of money, even with my scholarships. You and dad didn't go to college, and you've done alright."

"Times are different now. We're just farmers, but you could make this place grow.

194

Who knows, maybe you'll decide you don't want to be a farmer or raise cattle like your dad."

"But I *do* want to be a farmer."

"Then go to college and learn to be the best farmer you can be. Learn all the new things your dad and I don't know. You're going to be fine."

She came around the table and gave her son a big hug. "Just promise you'll never get too smart or too big that your mom can't hug you once in a while."

This made him smile.

She turned away so Jesse wouldn't see the tears building in her eyes. She pushed them away and called over her shoulder, "You had better get going before your dad comes looking for you."

Ted stood in the doorway with his arms crossed over his chest. He watched Jesse get up and push the chair back under the table. His smile read as a man who was very proud of the boy who stood almost his own height.

"Ready, Jesse?" he asked. "We have cattle and chickens to feed. I need to check the hives for mites, as well as the honey production. There are still a lot of blooming plants for the bees to feed on."

Jesse joined him and headed for the door.

"I'm pleased Jim was able to leave us a couple of hives. Maybe we can get a split or two in time." Ted grabbed his baseball cap off the peg by the door and walked down the porch steps. The dogs happily followed behind.

Jesse enjoyed working with his father on the farm. He and Katy would make good farmers, just like his mom and dad. They discussed it often during their nightly phone calls.

"Jesse, I'm afraid Brice will get off somehow and come after us again,"

"I don't think there's a chance in hell that'll happen. Think of all the evidence there is against him. The pictures of what he did to you and all the statements from the other girls proving what he is really like. He'll get jail time alright."

"I hope you're right." They said goodnight.

The next morning Jesse heard the phone ring.

"I'll get it. It might be Katy," he called out. "Hello?"

"Jesse, is your mom or dad around?"

"Dad, it's for you," he shouted. As Tom reached for the phone Jesse whispered, "It sounds important.

"Yes?"

"Mr. Sullivan, this is Matthew Coffee with the DA's office calling from Tampa. I wanted to let you know that there's been another incident. Another girl has brought charges against Bachlund. The boy went back home yesterday to meet with his attorney. Last night he beat up a girl named Cassie Moore. I believe they had been dating. She is so bad her doctor transported her to Manatee Memorial in Bradenton. She has a broken nose, a concussion and several broken ribs. Witnesses told the police he kicked her repeatedly. They pulled him off and called the police. He's under arrest and will be held without bail this time. This can only strengthen our case. I just wanted you to know."

"I can't believe Brice is so stupid!" Tom said when he hung up.

Doris and Jesse were eagerly awaiting details.

"Brice is back in jail. He attacked another girl last night."

After the call the house became unnaturally quiet. Ted went into the bedroom where Doris was dusting the furniture. He walked up behind and wrapped his arms around her.

"Everything is going to work out. Our kids are safe as long as Brice is in jail. He *will* be convicted and spend much of his life in prison, then we can all get on with our lives."

Chapter 27

"Barry, how about another piece of pie?"
the older woman asked. She took his plate
and added a slice before he had time to
swallow.
"Yes, please, ma'am. This sure is good pie.
Maybe someday you can give my wife pie
making lessons," Barry laughed.
"Are we keeping you from your family?"
Josh asked Barry.
"My Deidra is playing bingo tonight at the
firehouse. She wins a little and loses more
than she wins, but she likes her evenings out
with her friends. Besides, I get called out at
all times of the day and night. She's good
about that too."
"Anybody want more before I put it away?"
Mrs. Sullivan asked. When no one responded
she put the rest in the fridge and gathered up
their other dishes. "You come by anytime,
Barry. I sometimes buy pies from the grocery,
but Jesse likes mine better."
Barry turned to Josh and with a mouthful
of pie asked, "You say Travis stopped by?"

"Yes. He didn't stay long but said he'd come by again in the morning."

"I don't think he stayed long enough," Barry mumbled, a quizzical look on his face.

Katy sat in her rocker and brought the bag of knitting from the floor. She carefully pulled out the nearly-afghan and knitting needles. Then she replaced the bag and settled in.

"Let's see, where was I..."

Chapter 28

The trial began the first week in September. The crowded courtroom was sweltering, in spite of the fans that had been placed around the room.

The bailiff called the room to order.

"Please stand for the Honorable Judge Walter H. Dexter."

As everyone complied Jesse took Katy's hand and squeezed it. "Here we go. Are you ready?"

"Yeah, I'll be fine. I just want it over quickly."

Brice glared at them from the defendant's table where he was seated with his lawyer. Max Sawyer, was a tall man with thinning hair and a very nice suit. Sawyer shuffled papers he drew out of the folders in front of him.

"He looks like he eats little children for breakfast," Katy said, holding onto Jesse and shaking visibly.

The two attorneys talked to the crowd summarizing the charges and explaining what they thought had happened and what they wanted to prove. Then witnesses were called for both sides to give their testimony. Each attorney had a chance to question them. As time passed Katy became less anxious.

"Do you swear to tell the truth..." Preceded each new witness, and then Jesse was called.

"Jesse, did you have an altercation on March 14th, with the defendant?"

"Yes, sir."

"Was it over some comments he made to Katy Hailey?" Mr. Coffee asked.

"Yes, sir. It was."

"Can you briefly describe the events leading up to that incident?"

"Objection," Sawyer shouted. "The question is not relevant."

"On the contrary, I'm laying a foundation for what happed later, Your Honor. And it will show that the defendant had a prior run in with Miss Hailey and Mr. Sullivan, which led to the evening in question."

"I'll allow it," the judge said.

"A bunch of us... well, 3 couples met up to go to the movies in Arcadia. Brice was making fun of my date and being crude. He was saying awful things about the girl I was with."

"Who was that girl you were with, Jesse?"

"Katy Hailey, sir."

"What kind of things was he saying?"

"Do I have to say?"

"Yes, I think the jury needs to know."

Jesse repeated the insults and insinuations that Brice had made that night.

"How did you react to this?"

"I hit him and knocked him down. I told him to never speak to her like that again."

"What did you do after that?"

"Katy and I got in my truck and left."

"Jesse, did Brice say anything after you hit him and when you were leaving?"

"He said he would get even. That no one hits him and gets away with it."

"Did you take his threat seriously?" Coffee asked.

"You bet I did. We all did. I felt like I had a target on my back.

"I have no more questions of this witness, Your Honor."

The defense attorney got up from his chair and went to stand in front of Jesse.

"Jesse, were any of the supposed accusations true?"

"No, of course not," Jesse raised his voice. "He didn't know her. He'd never met Katy before that night."

"Just answer the questions 'yes' or 'no'."

"Did Miss Hailey have a reputation at school that would make him think that she was what he called her?" Sawyer asked.

"No."

"Is there a chance that you just didn't hear of her reputation?"

"No. She didn't even go to our school."

"I have no more questions at this time, Your Honor, but I reserve the right to call him again."

Jesse returned to his seat beside Katy.

"You should see the faces of the jury! I don't think they like Brice right now," Katy whispered.

Janice was called next.

"Please state your name for the court," Coffee began.

ADA Coffee was gentle but thorough in his questioning. Janice broke down several times during her questioning. Through her tears she was able to give her account of the rape.

Sawyer was less gentle. He took aim and tried to make it seem that she had consensual sex with Brice.

"No! I didn't! Are you saying I volunteered to get beat up and raped!"

"Oh, my gosh, Jessie. He is being so hard on her," Katy said, as she twisted and untwisted her handkerchief.

"Why didn't you come forward after the attack?" Sawyer asked, turning smugly to the jury.

"I was embarrassed. I didn't want people to know! What would they think? What would they say?"

"Isn't it true you wanted Brice Buchlund, the rich boy at school? If you got pregnant you'd marry all that money. Isn't that true?"

"I object, Your Honor." Coffee jumped out of his chair. "He's badgering the witness."

"Mr. Sawyer, you know better," Judge Dexter rebuked him.

Mr. Coffee called Cora to testify to the bruises Janice received and her refusal to return to school and facing Brice.

"Please tell the jury what you saw when you visited Janice's house that day."

"She was terrified of Brice," she began.

Hank was called to substantiate what the girls had claimed at that time.

Mr. Coffee asked each witness what Brice was like in school. How he acted afterwards. Why they felt he had no remorse? "

"Brice was bragging to all his friends. He *likes* hurting girls!" Hank said, jumping to his feet and pointing directly at Brice.

There was an audible gasp heard around the courtroom followed by murmuring.

"Order in the court." Dexter rapped his gavel.

"Objection!" Sawyer shouted. "It calls for speculation."

"The jury is directed to disregard that statement." Dexter ordered.

Coffee was pleased. He knew the jury wouldn't forget the energy leading to that dramatic moment.

Katy walked to the witness box, visibly shaking. She tried to keep her head clear, after all, the trial was about her standing up to Brice. She was doing this for all the girls he hurt and to prevent him from ever doing it again. He had to be held accountable for all the hurting. Being brave was new to her, but she gained strength from Jesse, and she would not let him down.

"State your name for the court, please." Coffee said.

"Katherine Marie Hailey."

She gave them details, told the truth, and only few tears moistened her cheek. She held her head high. The defense attorney could not deny that her testimony would bury his client.

When she finished, she walked steadily back to Jesse; all fear was gone and she felt more confident.

Jesse squeezed her hand as she sat down beside him. He leaned over and whispered, "I'm so proud of you."

Malinda, sitting behind her, leaned forward and patted her on the back. Doris and Ted smiled at her and she could read the pride in their eyes, and she peeked at Jim, who beamed proudly.

The trial took three days, but the jury was only out an hour. Everyone was called back into the court room.

"All rise... this court is now in session. The Honorable Walter H. Dexter presiding." the bailiff called. The calling of the jury brought everyone to their feet again.

"The defendant will rise and face the jury," Judge Dexter ordered.

Brice stood with his attorney. Mr. Buchlund sat in the crowd. The foreman handed the verdict to the bailiff, who handed it to the judge, who read it and handed it back.

"Men and women of the jury, how do you find?"

The courtroom went so still only the oscillating fans could be heard.

"We the members of the jury," said the jury foreman, "find the defendant guilty of assault and attempted rape."

"Thank you, ladies and gentlemen of the jury. You are dismissed," Judge Dexter decreed. "We will meet back here tomorrow morning at nine am when I will pronounce sentence."

The courtroom came alive with jubilation; girls crying with joy and congratulating one another. Jim Hailey clapped Coffee on the back and thanked him twice, and then was completely at a loss for words. Malinda hugged Katy. Janice wept but the smile never left her face. Hank hugged Cora and shook his fists in the air in triumph.

Only Mr. Sawyer saw the reaction on the face of his client. Brice did not react at first then turned to his attorney.

"I will find you one day when you least expect it and on that day you will die." He

spoke so softly that even his father didn't
hear him. The older Bachlund sat behind him
in the courtroom, with his hands covering his
face, rocked back and forth asking, my God,
how did this happen?

Chapter 29

The next morning the families gathered at the court house early and were in their seats by eight-forty-five. The wait for the bailiff and judge was torment. Finally, officers brought Brice into the courtroom with his attorney and followed by his father. Mr. Bachlund appeared to have aged ten years overnight. The bailiff called the room to order, and everyone stood while the judge took his place.

"Will the defendant please stand."

Brice stood and faced the judge. His hands were clasped behind his back, his feet apart, as though he were at ease. No expression or glimmer of response would give away his thoughts or feelings.

"I have watched this defendant throughout this trial, heard the charges brought against him and heard the numerous witnesses who know him. The evidence herein displays a destructive and vindictive cruelty. The defendant has offered no remorse or regret for his acts. He contributes a wantonly cruel nature. After considerable deliberation, it is the will of this court that the defendant, Brice Bachlund, be sentenced to fifteen years in the state prison. If it were up to me, the sentence would be longer as the pattern of behavior presented by this young man is habitual and without cause. Please take Mr. Bachlund into custody."

Brice was led out of the courtroom in handcuffs. Mr. Bachlund sat motionless. He was pale and seemed he might pass out at any moment.

Katy walked up and put her hand on his shoulder, "I'm sure you did the best you knew how, Mr. Bachlund. I'm sorry it turned out this way."

Jesse took Katy's hand and drew her away to join their parents. It was a long drive back home. Relief from all the stress that had built over these past six months left everyone feeling empty, as if all their blood had drained away. It would take a while to renourish them. Like the bees in the fire, their lives had been tainted, but now living without fear would gradually settle and in time everything would be better.

Matt Coffee called the Sullivans in the second week in December.

"Tom, I thought you'd like to know that Cassie Moore's trial has ended with Brice Bachlund receiving an additional ten years to serve. Cassie, it seems, was only fifteen and therefore still a minor."

"Mr. Bachlund sold his dealership and left the area. I guess the shame was too much for him," Tom said.

"That's about it for now. If you need anything, give me a call. Hope you folks have a pleasant holiday."

Ted hung up the phone and sat down on the stairs, "Coffee says Brice gets another ten years for that little Moore girl.

"Let's hope that's the end of it," Doris said as she sat down beside him.

"Let's hope," He said and put his arm around her.

Chapter 30

The next few years were busy ones for the Sullivans and Haileys. After college Jesse married Katy at St Anthony of Padua in North Port Charlotte where her Dad and Malinda had married.

Their reception turned out to be the perfect dance Jesse had promised. Katy asked Jesse to wear the crown as they danced the first dance at the reception. He smiled and complied, but it was removed immediately afterward.

The couple moved in with Ted and Doris and helped worked the farm. New techniques in breeding and raising cattle brought a major improvement and the farm prospered.

Jesse and Katy gave birth to three healthy and rambunctious children, Danny, Helen and James Theodore were born two years apart. Katy had help. Doris and Malinda were a constantly around and naturally spoiled the children. They followed Ted and Jesse around the farm and were soon helping with the cattle, chickens and bees.

The family and farm flourished as the years raced by. Jesse and Katy became grandparents. Danny had three boys. Helen had two girls and a boy, and J.T. gave them a girl and then a boy.

Although not financially, they did suffer hardships. When cancer claimed Ted at age 60, it left Doris devastated. He was buried near his parents in the small family cemetery behind the orange grove. Doris followed him the next spring. Windblown blossoms from the nearby orange trees covering her grave comforted Jesse and Katy. It was a pleasant reminder that the two, who loved one another so deeply in life, were now together again in spirit.

Malinda caught pneumonia in the winter of 1977, and passed away quietly at home. Jim continued his apiarist business. He taught his grandchildren candle making and now to keep the bee yard free of litter and crawling nuisances. He cherished his grandchildren and one day he became a great-grandpa. Soon afterward Jim went to live at Honey Tree Farm.

"How's your dad?" Jesse asked one afternoon as he came into the kitchen from the feed lot. "Maybe he'd like to take a walk in the grove before dark."

"It's a nice evening, he might enjoy that. You've got a while before sunset and we won't eat for a while. Go ask him."

Jesse returned and stopped in the doorway. He was white as a sheet and Katy knew by the look on his face. "It's Dad..." It wasn't so much a question as a statement.

"Yeah, it must have been quick. He still had the crossword..."

She dashed past him and into the living room. Jim looked comfortable in his chair, puzzle in his hand and his glasses on. He looked like he had just dozed off for a minute." Katy walked over and touched his cheek. She leaned down and kissed him.

"I never heard a thing. I took him tea a while ago. He didn't even finish it."

Katy turned into Jesse's arms. She hugged him fiercely. She didn't want to cry. Jesse kissed the top of her head.

"I had a feeling at lunch when he didn't eat much. He just said he was a little tired. But he seemed to be winding down lately, like a clock running out of time." She buried her face in his shirt, gave in and softly wept. Jesse held Katy, his own throat ached and tears formed.

Jim was buried, according to his wishes, in Myakka next to Katy's mother and Malinda. Katy visited the grave site often at first.

"I know it's probably strange to some that both my mom and Malinda are buried here with my dad, but he loved them both and it seems right somehow."

"It is what they wanted and that is all that matters. You've had so many people love you, Katy, including me. I'm so glad you came to the farm that day." He took her hand and kissed it. Hand in hand they walked back to the car.

The extra leaf in the old dining room table was in constant use now that Teddy, his wife Alice and the grandkids came on Sundays for dinner. Their youngest, Travis, shadowed Jesse on every visit. Jesse answered all his questions and gave him jobs to do. The dirtier he got, the happier the boy was. The years seemed to fly by, but the one thing in that held his interest was the bees.

One Sunday in March 1996, Travis and Grandpa Jesse were walking through the orange grove. The orange blossom perfume was almost over-powering and the only sounds were the bees buzzing, birds chirping and leaves rustling in the light breeze.

"Grandpa, when can I have my own hive?"

"Let's see. How old are you now, twelve?"

"Grandpa, I'm sixteen! I'll graduate high school next year."

"Why don't we find some queens and make a couple of splits. That will get you started."

"Why can't I have a brand new one? You know, start one from the beginning? My

214

birthday's in a couple of weeks. I'd like my
own bees and my own hive. Please, Grandpa?"
"Well, I'll look into it, but no promises."
Jesse never made promises he couldn't keep.
"I'll call Ben Jacobs at the Feed and Grain
store in Zolfo Springs. We need to get some
prices together, and see how long it would
take to get a new hive and have the bees
shipped in."
"Thanks, Grandpa. I'll work extra hard
around the farm to pay you back."
"It's not a done deal yet. Don't go getting
ahead of yourself," Jesse said, and patted the
boy's shoulder. "Sixteen, huh? That's why you
look hungry; let's go see if Grandma has any
of that Rhubarb pie left."
Jesse talked it over with Katy, but she
was less enthusiastic.
"Are you sure he's ready for his own hive?
You know how kids are. They want something
badly and then lose interest once they have it
a while."
"Not a problem. If he loses interest, what's
the worst that can happen?"
"We have another hive to care for."
"Right, and if he sticks with it, he learns
responsibility and will earn money from the
honey."
"Okay, call Ben and set it up. I'll get
with Teddy and Alice and work out plans for
his birthday. Do you think we can we get it all
in time?" Katy said, as she counted off the

days until Travis's birthday at a calendar on the back of the kitchen door.

"I'll know more after I talk to Ben." Jesse said. He took a cup of coffee and sat on the stairs to make his call. "Katy, we really need to get a longer cord for this phone."

"You say that every time, but you never do anything about it," Katy laughed, as she passed him on the steps, her arms full of folded laundry for the upstairs closet.

Back in the kitchen a few minutes later, she sat started a shopping list. At the top she wrote <u>longer phone cord</u> and underlined it.

"Ben doesn't know if the bees will arrive in time," Jesse said, as he came back into the room. "He has one more new hive at the store. I'll pick it up today. Ben said something else... Brice is in town."

"I thought he moved to Texas when he got out? What is he doing here? Well, I don't care." Katy fingered the shopping list. "Why don't I ride with you? You can drop me off at the grocery. We need some things and you can get the hive for Travis." She grinned up at him. "I know you, you'll talk to everyone at Ben's, and the supper and I will get cold waiting for you."

"Don't be silly," he kissed her on the cheek and took the list. I won't be long."

Chapter 30

The headlights bounced on the pavement as the tow truck lumbered along the country road. It carried three passengers and a broken rental car. All was quiet until Josh broke the silence.

"Thanks for helping me move the rocker back to the porch."

Barry just nodded.

"I guess you haul a lot of cars out of ditches around here," Josh said, in an effort to fill the silence.

"A fair few, yep." Another long silence followed and then Barry said, "Sorry Miz Sullivan couldn't finish her story."

"I'm sorry, too. But we couldn't stay any longer. You could see how tired she was getting. I hope her husband appreciates her waiting up for him like this," said Maggie, with a little edge in her voice.

"She's been waiting for him to come home for near twenty years or about that," Barry replied.

Maggie and Josh were stunned.

"What do you mean? She kept saying he was coming home tonight." said Maggie.

"She's been doing that practically every night since the accident, ma'am."

"What accident?" Maggie turned to Barry.

"Well, you no doubt heard about Brice and how he blamed them for messing with him and how they ruin't his life. He never figured anything was his fault. I was a young man back then. Shoot, everyone round here knew the story."

Barry removed his cap and scratched his head, then put the cap back again. "Travis wanted a hive of his own. Well, Jesse went to Ben's to pick it up and, don't you know it, that Brice was right there at the store. He'd done his time and stayed away for years. Don't know what possessed him to come back. Anyways, Jesse finished loading up his truck and was 'bout to go when Brice stepped up, blocking him. I know all this 'cause I saw it.

"Deidra and me had some ducks back then, and I'd gone to get some cracked corn for 'em. She had me pick up some crushed oyster shells too. You know, duck eggs will have a soft shell if you don't feed 'em crushed oyster shells? She even had me put in a kiddy pool for them to swim in. I had a lot of duck dinners in my future," Barry laughed.

"Barry, what about Brice and Jesse?" Josh said.

"Oh yeah," he began again, "Brice was all hopped up. He'd been drinking. He's strutting around acting all tough and surly. He sees Jesse and stumbles over to him.

"Well, lookie whose here." he says poking his finger at Jesse's chest. But Jesse stands his ground.

"Little early in the morning to be tying one on, isn't it?"

"Ol' Brice, he looks at Jesse and spits. He just missed the toe of Jesse's boot.

"You got a problem with how I enjoy myself, Jesse? Seems you've always had a problem with how I live my life; yes sir, for as long as I can remember.'

"I only had a problem with how you living your life affects other people."

"Heard you married that whore of yours?"

"That was the wrong thing to say to Jesse. He hauls off and hits Brice a good one, right on the jaw. 'en just like in the old days, Brice goes down like a ton a bricks. That man could never take a punch. Jesse steps over him, gets in his truck and drives off. I saw Brice stumble to his truck and take off after him. The rest I heard from the police and what the papers said."

Barry scratched his head as if trying to remember.

"What they put together is, Brice got in his truck and went after Jesse and chased him most of the way home. Brice tried to run him off the road. He slammed into the back of Jesse's, then pulled alongside to force him into a ditch. Jesse's Dodge had gouges and paint on it from Brice's truck.

"Brice caught up with him about a mile from home. He broadsided him. They figured Jesse spun around a couple of times before catching the side of the ditch. He was going so fast he flipped over about eight times and landed in old man Culver's cow pasture. Jesse was thrown clear, but he didn't have a chance. By the time they got anyone out there he was gone."

"Oh, my God," Maggie had tears in her eyes. Josh sat there stunned.

"I was called to get the truck out of the field. It was a terrible sight," Barry said.

They had reached an intersection and Barry stopping for a red light.

"What about Brice?" Josh asked.

"He was able to limp home, somehow. His truck was there too. It was pretty beat up, as you can imagine. The police found Brice a few days later holed up in an old barn out by the Desoto Speedway. He was messed up too. He spent a few days in the hospital before they dragged him to jail."

"How was Mrs. Sullivan when they told her that Jesse was dead?"

"That was the strangest thing. I called Travis and told him first. We wanted to be the ones to tell her before the cops came. She had supper all laid out on the table in the kitchen. Travis went in first and had her to sit down.

"Grandma, I have some bad news for you." He pulled out a chair sat beside her. "It's about Grandpa. He's had an accident with the truck. It's bad. I'm sorry, Grandma, Grandpa's dead."

"Don't' be silly, Travis," Katy got up and walked to the sink. She started washing a cooking pot. Her back to us, she asks, "You two want to stay for supper? We have plenty. Barry you have to bring your Deidra by sometime. She's such a nice girl." Then she turned and headed out to the porch to look for Jesse.

"Jesse, are you out there? Supper is getting cold." The dogs ran around the yard looking for Jesse.

"Miz Sullivan, It's true. I saw the wreck myself. Jesse had a run in with Brice and ended up crashing in Culver's cow pasture. He died before help arrived."

"Thanks for coming round, Barry. Travis, supper is on the table. Are you boys staying or not?"

"Grandma, do you understand what we told you?" Travis took her by the shoulders and looked her straight in her eyes. He could see she wasn't there.

"Barry, I think she's in shock. Call Dr. Farrell. Tell him what happened and ask him to come out, please." Barry went to the phone in the hall and did as he was asked.

Travis could hear me talking to the doctor and tried to get his Grandma to sit down. She wouldn't.

"I'll fix us a nice cup of tea, okay? You get the cups." She filled the kettle with water.

Travis reached in the cupboard and got out three mugs.

"Travis," she said, "We'll need four cups. I imagine he'll be along soon."

"I left when the doctor came. Miz Sullivan attended the funeral, but had this glazed look. She said to me how strange it was that Jesse missed the funeral.

"Doc Farrell said she'd come around one of these days and to just be patient. But she's been like that ever since. She's the sweetest, most generous person I know, but she still believes that Jesse is coming home back."

"Oh, the poor thing, to lose him like that," Maggie patted her nose with a Kleenex.

"Well, folks, we are just about there," Barry hit the turn signal, the left green light blinked on.

"There are my parents," said Josh, pointing.

Barry pulled into the lot and put the truck in park. The three climbed down and stretched their legs.

"Well, folks, it was nice to meet you,"
Barry extended his hand. Josh thanked him.
Maggie grabbed his hand and squeezed it.

"Please. Will you let us know how Mrs.
Sullivan is doing once in a while?"

They heard the Beaumonts chattering as
they approached.

"It's just that after hearing her story..."
Maggie couldn't go on, but Barry knew what
she meant even without the words.

Chapter 31

Mrs. Sullivan was restless after everyone left. The company was wonderful, but she was used to less excitement. There was nothing to do in the kitchen. She was tired but didn't want to go up to bed just yet. At the screen door she called the dogs and let them in.

"Why don't we sit on the porch for a spell," she said to them. Tucker got a drink and Blue curled up on the floor beside her. "He'll be along soon."

She gathered up an afghan to throw over her shoulders and took a seat in her old rocker. Bella jumped into her lap.

The light from the three-quart moon shown over the farm she had come to love, and the smell of orange blossoms filled the air.

"This is the best time of the year isn't it?" She sighed deeply.

"It surly is." She heard him say.

"Well, it's about time, Jesse. I didn't hear you come up."

"I figure you've been waiting long."

He took her hand as he sat at the table beside her.

"What kept you so long?" she scolded.

"I had to wait for you to finish your story.

"Well, you're here and that's what matters." She closed her eyes and took a breath of the heady orange blossom atmosphere.

You rest now, my Katy. Your story has come to its end."

She smiled and sighed one last time.

Epilogue

Josh and Maggie never did make it back to Honey Tree Farm before they returned to Atlanta. In their condo Maggie unpacked while Josh sorted through the pile of mail they had picked up from the post office.

"Maggie, here's a letter from Florida. It's postmarked Arcadia." Josh handed it to her.

She tore the envelope open and took out the single sheet of paper. Tears welled up as she read the short note. Unable to speak, she handed it to Josh.

As he read it, his voice shook with emotion.

Dear Maggie and Josh,

I'm sorry to tell you that my Grandma passed away during the night the day you left.

The next morning, when I went to check on her she was in her rocker on the porch. It was sudden and peaceful. She had the most wonderful expression on her face. She always said that her Jesse would come home to her, and I believe that he did that night.

I know she enjoyed her company and her story. She would want you to know.

Sincerely,

Travis Sullivan

"Oh Josh," Maggie sniffed, "She was such a sweet woman."

Josh held Maggie in his arms.

"I was thinking," Josh began. "Do we have to wait until Thanksgiving and have a big church wedding here in Atlanta? What if we had a small church wedding in a month or so?"

"Josh, have you been reading my mind again?" Maggie smiled.

In early May, Josh and Maggie stood on the steps of a little white church in Myakka. There before parents, friends, Barry and Deidra, Travis and his family, they heard the preacher say, "I now pronounce you man and wife and you may kiss the bride."

HONEY TREE FARM

Keep reading for an excerpt from

Broken Branches

By

Brenda M. Spalding

BROKEN BRANCHES

Broken Branches

A mystery by
Brenda M. Spalding

Chapter 1

"Okay, Gran, I promise. I'll come up to Salem this weekend for sure," Megan said, perched on the corner of her mother's old antique desk—her long legs dangling over the side.

She glanced at her calendar and thought about all she had to arrange for her art gallery to function in her absence. Her assistants were great; she just had to make sure they knew what needed to be done. After all, it would be only for a weekend. Today was Tuesday the fifteenth—the Ides of October. She frowned, hoping that wasn't a bad omen. No, there was plenty of time to get things organized.

Megan had a growing reputation as a brilliant watercolorist. She had a classroom/studio in the back, and her classes were always full—with a waiting list of students trying to get in.

"Sorry to cut this short, Gran, but I have a lot to do if I'm going to take time off for a visit. I should have planned to visit before now."

"Yes, dear, I know how busy you are with the gallery and all. But I've *got* to talk to you about something. It really can't wait any longer. I'm not getting any younger, and there are things you need to know. I need your help, and I'd rather just…" Gran's voice trailed off.

"Gran, are you there?" Only silence answered Megan for a moment.

Then Megan's grandmother whispered into the phone, "I heard something upstairs." She paused to listen. Lately she'd heard a lot of strange sounds in the old house. The house had been in her family for generations.

"Sorry, I thought I heard something again."

"What do you mean 'again?' Gran, what did you hear?"

"Got to go! See you soon!"

Megan stared at the unresponsive phone in her hand. "What the hell was that all about?" she shrugged.

Megan went back to work on the papers before her. Later she called her grandmother back but got no answer. Megan was a bit concerned after their last conversation but she knew Gran had friends she often went out with. She made a mental note to try again later.

"Now for these invoices, or I'm not going anywhere. I really do need to hire a bookkeeper." Megan said to an empty room. She busied herself with paperwork and the business of running a successful gallery for the rest of the day. In between she looked up flights from New York to Boston, checking times and prices. All the while, disturbing questions about her grandmother and the strange ending to their conversation invaded her thoughts.

*****

Megan's grandmother hung up the phone and stood there, listening, waiting to see if the sounds she had heard would repeat. *I must be losing it for real*, she thought.

Then she heard it again, a noise like furniture being dragged across the floor. It was coming from the attic above her. Quietly and as quickly as she could manage, she pulled herself up the stairs using the handrail. She stopped on the landing to catch her breath and listened again. She hadn't been upstairs much in the last few years.

There it was again. *Definitely the attic*, she assured herself. Reaching the top of the stairs, she walked down the hallway and eased open the attic door. She was positive someone was up there. Deciding to go down and call the police she turned, caught her foot on the carpet and bumped her elbow hard on the door frame—sending a painful zing up her arm.

"Ow! Damn, that hurt," she whispered, hoping her stifled exclamation hadn't been heard in the attic. She held her breath and

Broken Branches

waited, praying she could get away before being caught.

Shuffling down the hall, she heard someone rushing down the attic stairs. She made it to the top of the stairs when she felt a hand grip her shoulder and shove her hard.

Chapter 2

The answer to Megan's unanswered questions came the next morning. Salem police called to inform her that Corey Elizabeth Bishop, Megan's grandmother, had been found dead at the bottom of her stairs.

She was sitting there trying to absorb what the police had told her when Megan's assistant, Jennifer, knocked on her office door. Walking in, she found her boss sitting behind her desk, softly crying. "Megan what's wrong?" she asked.

"That call was from the Salem police up in Massachusetts. My grandmother had an accident at home and died. I can't believe it. I only talked to her yesterday. You know I told you I was planning to go up this weekend. I've not visited her in a while, and she had something to tell me." Megan choked out between sobs while wiping her tears. "I knew she was getting on, but I didn't think she was that bad."

Megan took a tissue from the box Jennifer handed her and took a deep breath. "Jen, I'm going to have to take some time off to deal with this. Oh, God, Jen, how do people do this? I can't even think straight right now."

"Don't worry about the gallery," Jennifer said. "You go take care of things up there. We'll take care of things here. Annie can handle the invoices. The current exhibition will be up for a few more weeks. By then you should be back."

Jennifer handed Megan more tissues, helped her with her coat and walked her out. "You have a good team here, and we can reach you on your cell if we have any questions." They hugged and Jennifer watched Megan walk slowly down the street.

She took the subway home lost in thought about the wonderful times she'd had at her Gran's house. As a child she had spent a couple weeks there every summer. Hand in hand they would walk the beach looking for the best shells to decorate the towering sand castles they built together.

Recalling those summers brought her parents to mind. Years ago, they had been killed by a drunk driver. A Sunday trip to the Hamptons, checking out a new gallery had made Megan an orphan.

Back in her apartment, she flopped down in a chair and cried again softly. The shock of the news was wearing off. She started making mental notes of all she needed to arrange. She spent time looking up funeral homes in Salem. She chose one and gave them a call. The director was wonderful and promised to take care of most of the details. Then she called Delta and booked a flight to Boston for the next day.

BROKEN BRANCHES

Bottle Alley

Its 1938, the carnival is in town and a hurricane is on the way. Driving rain and floods create havoc in the small community as the hurricane races closer.

The winds howl and cultures clash when Michael Flannigan falls for beautiful Russian fortune teller, Dania. Oldest child in a strong Irish family, Michael must prove himself to his family and to Dania's stubborn father, Boris Koslov.

Local lad, Johnny Russo is found dead in Silver Lake and the police suspect someone from the carnival is involved. The killer is on the run. Will he escape both the police and the forces of nature?

The carnival will move on but the 'The Lake' area of Newton, Massachusetts, will be changed forever.

The young locals have picked up the language of the carnivals and made it their own. 'The Lake Language is now a proud tradition passed down through the families and is still in use today.

Acknowledgements

I wish to thanks my editor Clarissa Thomasson for her help in the editing and formatting process. I could not have finished this book without her. I know I drove her crazy.

I also wish to thank my friend and fellow author Nancy Buscher who did a lot of hand holding and advising. Thanks for being there and for all your support

Author Brenda Spalding was raised in Newton, Massachusetts. She traveled for many years with her military husband before settling in Bradenton, Florida.

Brenda is a member of the National League of American Pen Women. She is the co-founder and current vice-president of ABCBooks4Children&Adults, Inc. ABC is a nonprofit 501c3 networking organization for local authors and illustrators.

She is the author of several children's books and three adult mainstream novels with more on the way.

Her children's books are meant to help the reader connect with the child and go beyond the book to explore the world around them.

Her mainstream books are developed using her love of her Irish heritage and the history of the area in which she is setting her story.

Made in the USA
Columbia, SC
01 March 2018